Heels Dug In

Astoria Wright

A Sassy Sleuth Mystery

Book 3

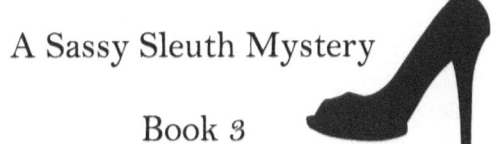

Heels Dug In

Published by Novelwright Press, LLC
Novelwright.com

Cover Art by James from GoOnWrite
GoOnWrite.com

Edited by 529Books
529Books.com

Table of Contents

Chapter 1

Mondragon Cruises

With the height of travel season on the horizon, I had a wardrobe to update. I hadn't taken a vacation in a year, and I wasn't going to miss the opportunity to soak up the sun somewhere outside of Diamond Springs, New York. It was too late to call it "spring cleaning," with summer half-way through, but my closet was undergoing a massive makeover. I was knee-deep in a pile of clothes I couldn't decide on keeping or tossing. It was hard to know what clothes might come in handy as an assistant to a private eye.

I nearly tripped over a bundle of dresses at the sound of my phone vibrating on the mid-level shelf. Wading through the pile, I reached the phone with my fingertips and checked the name on the caller ID.

Lizzy Mondragon.

Why would an old classmate from Lady Ashdale's Academy be calling me now? Not only had we lost touch since boarding school seven years ago, but we'd never really been in touch in the first place.

Every girl in Ashdale's came from wealthy families, me included. But the Mondragons were no mere millionaires. Somewhere in their family history, there were nobles. And they'd invested their wealth heavily in businesses that only seemed to grow with each generation. Lizzy Mondragon was the heiress to Mondragon International: a global chain of hotels, nightclubs, and a cruise line. As such, she did not socialize with any but the richest girls. She did once confide in me that she had doubts about the sincerity of their friendship. Still, her wealth placed expectations on her that made choosing her friends a luxury she couldn't afford. She strove to fulfill her parents' expectations, but she was as level-headed as any girl I'd met inside or outside of Ashdale's. If she hadn't been a year older than me, and I hadn't come from a Wall Street lawyer and an architect, we might have been friends.

"Hello?" I answered tentatively.

"Kait? Is this Kaitlynn Sasse of Diamond Springs?"

"Yes, Lizzy, it's me. How are you?"

"Relieved that Ella had the right number. Kait, I'm sorry I haven't kept in touch all these years."

Confused at the urgency in her voice, I said, "No worries. I know you have a lot on your shoulders."

The last I'd heard of Lizzy, she'd taken over Mondragon Cruise Line as her first step in preparing to run the Mondragon entrepreneurial empire. No one would blame her for not keeping in touch with old friends. I only hoped she'd had time to make new ones. I hadn't expected Ella to be on that list. Then again, knowing Ella, she'd done everything she could to secure a spot in Lizzy's address book.

"I know I shouldn't be calling out of the blue with a request, but Ella said you and your partner were the best private investigators in all the Northeast."

I'd have argued all the East Coast was more accurate, but I was speechless upon hearing that Ella had said anything good about me at all. She and I had gotten along better in recent weeks, but years of her competitiveness had strained whatever friendship we'd had in boarding school.

She might have had good things to say about PI Aeson "Ace" East. Her flirtations with him had gone unreciprocated until she'd finally gotten the message that Ace was interested in me, not her. Her backing off was an olive branch, and I took it as a step forward in our becoming friends again. But as hopeful as I'd been that Ace and I would move forward after that, he'd taken three steps back. Though Lizzy used the word "partner," the truth was Ace was my boss. As such, he was uncomfortable with a relationship between us.

I explained to Lizzy, "I work for a private eye. I don't actually have my license yet, but he's the best."

Or he would be until I got my results on the New York State Private Investigator Exam. I'd taken it earlier this month and was waiting to find out my score any day now. I was sure I'd aced it. After that, it was a trial period doing detective work side by side with Ace, then I'd finally be able to call myself a PI in my own right. My hope was for a partnership with Ace, and as much as I'd love a romantic one, a professional one would have to do.

Lizzy didn't notice or care about my status as a PI-in-waiting. She said, "I need the best right now, Katie."

Lizzy had only ever called me "Katie" when she was feeling vulnerable. Whatever was wrong, it was enough to shake a woman who'd been trained to hold her emotions in like a dam against water.

"What's happened?" I asked.

"Four women have gone missing on our biggest ship, *Fire on the Sea*, in the last six months."

"Missing? Do you think they were taken, or were they drowned?"

"We don't know. The disappearances weren't noticed until the re-boarding after the stop on the island. We've had our own security looking into it, and we've been cooperating with officials on the islands, but we can't find a trace of the girls anywhere."

"Which island?"

"Our new most popular destination site. It's a little-known island near Bermuda where we have a Mondragon resort. We're building a water park called Surfing Dragon there, but we haven't opened that up yet. There's only two companies who have resorts there and three cruise lines that visit, but we're in negotiation to buy the second resort and make the island a Mondragon International exclusive vacation spot."

"So if the women are being taken, there's a chance the island officials will blame Mondragon International."

"Exactly. The island and the water park are my ideas; I'm investing millions. If they close it down, it won't just mean a loss of money for the Mondragon company. My father will never trust me again. I can't lose my standing on the board."

Lizzy's voice wavered. I pictured her hands shaking and her shallow breathing like I'd seen during the time she had a panic attack in our last year at Lady Ashdale's. My fingertips numbed, perhaps from my grip on the phone. I knew what losing her position in the company meant to the Mondragons. Her father might as well disown her.

"Please, Katie. I had to call all the missing women's parents personally to tell them about their disappearances. I don't think I could stand to make another call. One of those girls, the last one to be taken, she was a crewmate on the *Fire on the Sea*. Her parents were so angry they threatened to launch a whole movement against the company."

"Did you inform the Coast Guard or the FBI?"

"It was international waters, so the local police and the British navy are investigating. I don't want the media here getting wind of this, you understand. I thought you and your boss could look into it. I'll give you an all-expense-paid cruise. Mid-summer, the cruises are packed, but we do have a honeymoon suite available. I know it's not ideal, but it would give you a cover. I don't want the cruise officials knowing that you're investigating. I don't know who's involved."

The desperation in her voice made it impossible to say no. Ace hated when I took on cases before consulting him, but I would soon have a license of my own. I should be taking the initiative. Besides, those families were suffering. Even if Lizzy's motivations may have been conflated with her company's goals, I knew she did care about what had happened to them.

"We'll take the case," I said.

"Thank you, Kait." Lizzy breathed an audible sigh of relief. "I'll send you the itinerary and meet you on the island with the details of the case. And, Kait, don't tell anyone—not even Ella. I never told her why I needed a PI. She thinks it's paparazzi-related paranoia, and I'd rather it stay that way. If the media gets wind of this before we make any progress investigating—"

"I understand."

With another deep exhale, Lizzy said, "You're a lifesaver."

Now all I had to do was tell Ace about our "honeymoon" plans.

Chapter 2

Trouble in Paradise

A ce grumbled under his breath as he loosened his tie. He could not have chosen a more conspicuous outfit than his blue blazer and dress pants. He looked pale, even with the tan he'd earned fishing on the lake behind his home. I'd have thought he was seasick just thinking about our ocean trip if I hadn't known that he loved the water and came from a naval family. Then again, Ace's was one of two families his father had been secretly keeping. Perhaps a journey on the ocean reminded him of that.

"Something wrong?" I asked as I hauled out my vintage floral rolling cart and bag set.

"Nope," Ace replied, grabbing them all in one swoop.

"Oh, no, you have my purse," I said, feeling the tug of the strap pulling away from my shoulder. I readjusted my coral colored maxi dress, retying the belt as Ace lifted the bags into the trunk one at a time.

"Too late. Have a seat, and I'll bring it to you in a second."

Feeling naked without my purse, I walked around to the passenger door of Ace's beaten-up Hyundai. I'd offered to drive my Bentley for the ride to Cape Liberty, but he said the miles wouldn't matter as much for his old car than my new one. He seemed to have cleaned up the interior, except for an old water bottle I'd found under the seat and the protein bar wrappers in the glove compartment. With his skills and salary as a PI, he could have afforded as good a car as mine, but he insisted on keeping a low profile.

I tossed the water bottle into a bin I'd bought him that he never seemed to use and stretched in preparation for the long ride to the Jersey shore. When he'd returned to the car and handed me my new summer purse, I said, "You never answered my question."

"Which question?"

I raised an eyebrow. For a man who could simultaneously follow three different conversations across a room and carry on one of his own, he wasn't on his game this morning. Since four lives might depend on us, I worried about what that meant for our case.

"Oh, is something wrong, you asked. No, nothing at all." He turned the ignition and crept down the road like a zombie. Staring at the pavement ahead, Ace kept his hands at ten and two and his mind somewhere far away.

The first hour of the commute, he drove like that. Tense and terse, he communicated in a series of "yesses," "nos," and indifferent "mmhmm's" that could barely be heard over the soft tunes playing in the background. When I finally clicked off the radio and asked him what was wrong, he glanced between the dashboard and me as if realizing for the first time he wasn't alone in the car.

I turned sideways in my seat, enough to feel my seatbelt pulling me back. "I know you were hesitant to take this case, but I didn't push you into it."

He shrugged. "Those missing girls have families. It's like you said, we have to help them if we can."

"So, why was your first answer to let the FBI handle it?"

"It's their jurisdiction."

"Firstly, that isn't true. It happened internationally, so the FBI isn't investigating. Secondly, private investigators don't have jurisdictions. So, why don't you tell me what's really on your mind?"

He sighed. "You remember I told you my father had…an unconventional family life."

I nodded slowly. I remembered the moment in Ace's living room when I had seen the navy medals and awards from his grandfather and father. The latter being a bigamist had come as a surprise. I recalled Ace's pained look when he'd shared that his father had kept a secret family in New Jersey, hours away from his home in Diamond Springs, New York.

"I have a half-brother. His name is Damian. I—we—don't speak, but I met him once. Back then, he was a troubled teen, especially after his dad, after our dad died. He took it hard."

"It must've been hard for both of you," I said.

Ace scratched his head, raising his eyebrows as if trying to keep any remote possibility of tears at bay. "Not really. I'd already lost him years before when we found out about his past."

"How did you find out?" I asked. I'd always been curious, but he'd never opened up like this before.

He laughed. "It was a private eye. That might be what drew me to this profession. I guess you could say, in a way, that my dad inspired my career. He did the same for my brother."

I tried making as light of it as he did, saying, "At least there's that. Did your brother become a private eye, too?"

"No. His inspiration was more literal. Dad was in the navy, and Damian went out to sea as well."

"He joined the navy?"

"Not exactly. He is the captain of a ship, though."

"Not the Fire on the Sea, I hope." The joke fell flat.

Ace took his eyes off the windshield long enough to look at me. I dropped the smile. He couldn't mean anything but that Damian East was captain of Mondragon's premier cruise ship.

"You're not serious?" I said.

"Deadly serious."

"Why didn't you tell me? I would have—"

"Would have what? Told your friend we can't help just because I might have to come face to face with my half-brother? It won't affect my ability to do my job."

"No, I understand. I'll be right there with you."

"Kait, I'm fine. I won't be mollycoddled by an overprotective assistant."

"Overprotective wife. Remember our cover story," I said, twirling the ring on my left ring finger, which was just a little big for my hand. I'd seen one in Zazbry's, but Ace was right that it was too expensive to buy just to go undercover. In the back of my mind, I hoped he took note of my taste in rings—for future reference. For all the details he kept in his mind, he couldn't seem to remember our fake marriage was our cover for this trip.

"Somehow, I don't think you'll let me forget," he said.

"Meaning?" My tone sharpened.

He sighed. "You know how I feel, but I think we ought to keep things professional, at least for now."

I wouldn't rebuff him for ending our relationship before it started. But his excuse that I ought to focus on my PI license was as fake as Ella Belle's nose. But I could see through Ace's reasoning better than I could spot a nose job.

"You're not comfortable with an employee/boss relationship. I get it, but you went from hot to cold like that." I snapped my fingers.

We had been getting hot, but before anything could really happen, Ace had turned to ice. We also went back to "Kaitlynn" instead of "Kait," and requests about filing instead of a little harmless flirting. While he'd returned to calling me by my nickname, eventually, he kept our relationship focused on one goal: my PI license. I knew I had to become full partner before he'd be comfortable resuming our romance, but I couldn't be as all-or-nothing about it as Ace.

I touched the ring around my finger as we reached our reserved parking spot at the pier. Did those four lost women have significant others? Did they have degrees, jobs, futures lined up for them after their cruises? Lizzy hadn't shared their information with me yet. But I wondered as the ship came into view who they were and whether they were still out there somewhere—fighting for their lives.

Ace stopped the car and turned to face me. Fumbling for something in his breast pocket, he seemed nervous. I raised an eyebrow, wondering if this was some kind of romantic gesture. Ace pulled out a box.

"Is that what I think it is?"

My heart skipped a beat. Jewelry? Nothing topped the ring on my finger, which had been Ace's grandmothers, but I'd take any heartfelt token of Ace's affections. My widening smile shrank before the next heartbeat.

Ace took out a slim, black, rectangular chip no larger than a mint. The blinking red light gave away its identity as a GPS tracker. He flipped it over to reveal a clip in the back.

"This is the best in tracker technology—at least in terms of what's on the market. You can clip it in your hair or on your clothes."

I took it reluctantly. It was light in my hand, but the weight of it sunk into my brain. We were investigating kidnappings, which put Ace and me in a rough spot. We weren't about to become the next victims.

Ace held up his phone, displaying a map with blinking yellow and orange dots near the cove. "I've got it set to transmit to my phone in case you're in trouble."

"Is your tracker on? I should program yours in, too," I said, taking my phone out of my purse.

Ace opened and closed his mouth, his expression full of surprise.

"You don't have a tracker, do you?"

He ran a hand through his hair. "The victims were all women."

"You're unbelievable. The victims may have all been women, but if anyone catches on that we're investigating, you'll be in danger too." I let out an exasperated sigh, then asked, "If you're not the other dot, who is?"

He hesitated. "Your primary tracker is in your purse. Since you never go anywhere without it, I thought...okay, I realize my mistake."

I shuffled through my purse, looking for the tracker. My cheeks grew hot as I searched.

"Never touch a woman's purse." I thrust the disk into Ace's hands. "And for your information, I did prepare a few safety precautions for this trip myself."

Then I motioned to drop the one he gave me into the bag. Ace's finger's closed over mine.

"Look, I'm sorry. But please keep one on you. I'll keep this one with me, see?" He slipped it into his jacket pocket.

I allowed a half-smile. "All right. Just as long as you realize I'm your partner in this investigation, not some damsel in distress. No more secretly tracking my whereabouts on the cruise, okay?"

He winced. "I probably should mention that I'm tracking your phone, too."

I jerked the door open with enough force to show I was angry. As Ace exited the vehicle, I clipped the tracker onto my belt and rolled my eyes. I knew I'd be fighting sea-sickness on this cruise, but I hoped I wouldn't be fighting Ace on this trip, too.

Chapter 3
Maritime Murder

I tried not to let Ace's faux pas bother me. It wasn't his fault that he wanted to be the protector. I recognized that it was sweet in the old-fashioned way of thinking. I also wanted him to realize that a soon-to-be PI had made her own preparations for a risky investigation. One thing I hadn't prepared for was Ace's long-lost half-brother being captain of the cruise ship.

I wouldn't know the first thing about siblings. I'd had friends who were close to their brothers and sisters, and those who often fought with them. I'd had a few fights with friends over the years, Ella Belle came readily to mind, but Ace's situation was no ordinary brotherly relationship. More than once, his eyes scanned the top of the boarding ramp. The captain wasn't visible yet.

Ace pried his eyes away from the ship as we checked in our luggage. A couple ahead of us held up the process. I caught snippets of their argument with security as I stretched my neck to see them.

The man wore a Hawaiian button-down and cargo pants. The woman had fastened a hat on her head with a sunflower hairpin and wore a lemon-yellow top with lime-green pants. The pair were middle-aged and matched each other in average height and build. The man reached for something in the suitcase, which security snatched away. Several heads turned in their direction, and the woman put a hand on her husband's shoulder as if becoming aware that they were making a scene.

The man ignored his wife and shouted in a Scottish accent, "It's just a bloody walking stick. I've got a bum knee, and you want to hobble a poor man on this trip?"

The security man held up a small container on a key chain—pepper spray, from what I could tell. The woman spoke more quietly than her husband, but I managed to make it out in the hush that had fallen over the immediate area. The woman said in a British accent, "It's just for protection."

Her husband shouted, "This is injustice over injustice." The security guard stepped closer, and the man jerked back. "No, I do not want to leave the cruise. Fine. We'll hand it over to you, but keep away from me."

An array of what must have been colorful words in Gaelic came out of his mouth as he left the luggage area and made his way for the ramp. I was too far away and too foreign to him to understand. In all my traveling, I hadn't encountered Scottish slang as much as other languages.

It didn't stop me from trying to puzzle out what the big row had been all about. I snapped out of it when Ace's hand gently nudged my upper back. We followed the couple to the boarding ramp. They were talking lower now, but I could hear them better close up.

"Please stop cursing at them, Glenn. Try and restrain yourself or you'll get us booted off."

"They can't understand me anyway, and I am restraining myself or I'd call them—"

He launched into a few words I did understand, and some I didn't. The woman's head quirked this way and that around the port nervously. I kept my eyes on my passport and ticket, trying not to be conspicuous about my eavesdropping.

We were only a few people behind them when the two finally reached the captain. Damian stood with his hands behind his back, giving greetings and welcoming passengers as they passed him onto the ship. Now that I could see him, I was struck by the resemblance. Captain Damian East was clean-shaven, no perpetual five o'clock shadow like Ace tended to have, with brown hair shades lighter than Ace's. I knew they were roughly the same age, but Damian looked older. His jawline was stronger than Ace's, and his build was that of a man who had seen the inside of a gym more days than Ace did. Despite my time around models, I'd never liked the overly-muscular type.

The angry passenger, Glenn, stuck his ticket out for Damian to see. Damian didn't seem to mind. He bore Glenn's point-blank stare with a friendly smile. After glancing at the ticket, Damian handed it back. Then, he outstretched his hand, which was covered in a white glove that seemed part of the uniform.

"Welcome aboard," he said.

Glenn refused to take the ticket or shake the captain's hand. He tapped the top of the paper where the name must have been listed. Leaning into Damian's personal space, Glenn said, "Roberts. Sound familiar?" His eyes darted around Damian's face as if analyzing every micro-expression.

Damian's eyes widened. A second later, he was oozing charm again. "It's a pleasure to have you aboard. If there's anything I can do for you, please don't hesitate to let me or my staff know."

"Oh, they'll know. If I find any problem aboard this ship, the whole world will know. Don't doubt it." He snatched his boarding ticket back and tugged at the rolling cart so that it clapped against the ramp.

Damian watched with narrowing eyes as the Roberts passed him. He didn't greet the next few people until we walked up to him. Ace was already face-to-face with Damian before he noticed we were there. He flashed the polite smile of sea captain, not seeming to recognize Ace. Perhaps because Glenn had so forcefully pointed out their names, Damian looked at the name on the ticket in Ace's hands. He clenched his jaw as his eyes slowly traveled upward.

Ace said, "Hello, Damian."

"Aeson."

"It's just Ace," he corrected.

Damian's eyes traveled over my face, and I swore he did a body check before glancing at my ticket, too. "Mrs. Kaitlynn...East?" He looked at Ace. "So, you're married now?"

I watched Ace for signs of flinching, reddening, shuffling, or any hint of discomfort at the idea of him and I as a couple. That had been his normal reaction lately.

Instead, he put his arm around my shoulders and drew me in. He didn't overplay it. He looked content as the corners of his mouth lifted ever so slightly. I loved that look. That was the look I imagined would cause wrinkles in his old age from many happy years.

"Yes, I am," was all he said. But the way he looked into my eyes—I had to be blushing.

I had to break my gaze to remember what we were doing here. I offered Damian my hand.

"It's a pleasure to meet you."

Damian looked at Ace before he shook my hand and uttered a quick, "Welcome aboard."

And that was that.

As Ace and I stepped onto the ship and walked up the stairs in search of our cabin, I held onto him. It was part of our disguise, but for me, it had a double meaning. I hoped Ace took it as *I know that was difficult for you, and I'm here as long as you need me.*

Chapter 4

Single Mingle

"Lizzy really didn't give you any information or case files for the missing women?" Ace asked when we received our bags from the porter. The "honeymoon suite" Lizzy had booked for us was the size of two regular cabins. It had a chaise lounge more than suitable for a bed for Ace to sleep on, as well as a king-sized bed for me. The vanity in the bathroom lit the space so brilliantly that my green eyes had to adjust before I could unpack. It had taken a few hours to get our luggage, but we both felt better now that we had settled in.

"Lizzy suspects the girls didn't go missing until they reached the island, so our real investigation begins then. Until then, we could just keep our eyes open for anything suspicious on the ship," I said, setting the curling iron in its place.

I came out of the bathroom to see Ace heaving the last of the luggage into the top shelf in the closet. Through his shirt, I could see the shape of his muscles, contracting and relaxing as he pulled his arms down. I looked away before he saw me staring.

"I still think we should've gotten them before we left. We have nothing to go on except the few internet articles I read, and they didn't disclose any details. We don't even know the name of the crewmate who went missing last month."

"Lizzy didn't want to have the files on an email record. She's trying to protect her company. We could try to find ship's security and ask a few questions as persnickety guests. Maybe sneak into the files." I loved thinking like a spy. I knew it was different in real life, but that didn't mean we couldn't use some James Bond-like tactics.

"I'm trying to protect our investigation. If we go around looking for ship's security, we give ourselves away to anyone who might be in on the kidnappings."

"So, we wait until we reach the island," I suggested. "We have a day and a half until then. What should we do with our first night aboard?"

Heels Dug In

Ace undid a button on his collar. I felt a thrill rush through me. The excitement faded as he walked right past me to the door and opened it.

"Mingle," he said.

I grabbed my purse and followed him out to the dining hall.

We chose a table near a wall positioned just right so we could view the entire dining area. Our conversation consisted of analyzing the types of people on board and which part of the dinner crowd could be targets or predators. I didn't see anything suspicious as we ate, except that I could count on one hand the number of times he looked at me.

"You're being too obvious," I said, taking a drink of the water in my wine glass.

That got him to look at me. "I am?"

I set down the glass and took his hand, smiling as a cover for my annoyance. "Whatever this distance thing is that we have going, it's not working for us looking like a couple. You're looking at everyone in the room but me, and you're a good enough investigator to know that's a dead giveaway."

He stared at me a moment. Then he said, "Maybe it was a mistake for you and me to come here as a couple."

My jaw dropped. I let go of Ace's hand. "Maybe it was."

Ace glanced at me and back in the direction he had been staring. "What I mean is, the four women who were taken were here alone. They might've been part of that party." He nodded in the direction of an area of the bar with a banner overhead.

Single Mingle, it read.

I realized what he meant. If the kidnapper was targeting single women, there was no better place to find them than a group like that. The kidnappers might be mixed into that crowd right now. In that case, we were too far out of the danger zone to spot them.

"We can't both go over there. People on board already know we're married." Of course, they might have assumed we were...an unconventional couple. But I preferred not to attract any extra attention. I was sure that would turn a few heads.

Ace replied, "No, but one of us should. Besides, we can cover more ground that way."

Ace was too much of a gentleman to ogle the single ladies at the bar. I didn't like the idea of him even trying. I popped out of my seat.

"I'll go," I said, throwing my napkin on the table. I tried to make it look like I was angry with Ace. It wasn't a far leap. I leaned close enough for him to hear me but kept my tone sharp, "Let people think we argued, and I stormed off."

"Fine."

I did not like how well he matched my tone, and it showed in the way I sauntered off to the singles area.

I walked straight to the bar. I wouldn't attract anyone with steam coming out of my ears and *back off* written all over my expression. So, I raised a hand to get the bartender's attention and order myself a remedy for my foul mood.

It didn't help that the bartender was busy. I figured I might as well use the wait time to scan the room. My eyes shot in the direction of a distressed woman's gasp, followed by an "*oh my god.*"

The source of the outcry downed a shot glass and tried, too conspicuously, not to look me in the eye. Naturally, I walked toward her. The moment I recognized her, my mouth went agape.

"Ella?"

Ella Belle hid her face with her hands. "Oh, god, this is embarrassing."

I sat at an open seat beside her and shrugged. "So, you're on a singles cruise. There's nothing wrong with that."

She straightened, turning to face me. Then she spotted my ring. I thought her eyes might pop out of her head.

She grabbed my fingers. "Who did you…?" She dropped my hand and said flatly, "It's Ace, isn't it?"

Ella looked like her stoic managerial expression might return, but within seconds, there were tears in her eyes.

"Ella, I—" I wanted to tell her that this was all a sham—that Ace and I were working a case—but that would break our cover. And, if I were honest, I had the added incentive of knowing that Ella drew the line at flirting with married men.

Ella raised her hand for another shot. "You don't have to say anything." The bartender set a glass down and started pouring. Her speech was slightly slurred and would only get worse after she downed whichever round of alcohol this was for her. "I'm happy for you. Really." She took a swig.

This was the worst I'd ever seen Ella…and the nicest she'd been in a long while. I was sorry to see her in such a state. It was worse because I wasn't sure if I was the cause of her distress or if it was because no one had approached her yet on this first night of the cruise. I found that hard to believe.

Heels Dug In

Despite the tipsy speech, Ella was objectively attractive. Her auburn hair fell in her face and she brushed it out of her blue eyes, retaining her posh proclivities even when drunk. Her clingy red dress showed off her body.

I tried hard not to picture Ace's reaction when he saw Ella on this singles section of the cruise. Would he see this vulnerable side of her and find out she had a heart? If he did, would he want to comfort her? Could he fall in love with her?

I shirked the thought and focused. There were a lot of men and women standing around chatting, sitting at tables getting cozy, and even a couple making out already. A handful of people stood shyly on the outskirts, looking for openings to approach people. Directly beside me was a group of women, seemingly content with each other's company and allowing interested men to come to them. That had always been my strategy.

Poor Ella must have come on the cruise alone. Certainly not something I would have done. But it was brave, too—unwittingly bold since there was every possibility the women on in this "Single Mingle" might be in danger. I split my attention between scouting the area for stalkers and listening to Ella's explanation of why she'd come. It was something about taking her first vacation in years and how her job as manager of the Blue Diamond Mall didn't allow her much time to socialize.

I nodded and gave an *"mm-hmm"* as the conversation required, but out of the corner of my eye, I'd caught a suspicious-looking man. He had black hair, stubble around his chin, and a black shirt and jeans on. Something about the way his eyes scanned the crowd made him stand out.

His eyes found Ella and me, and he didn't look away when I made eye contact. He didn't approach, either.

Ella hiccupped, drawing my attention back to her. She put a hand to her head and swerved in her seat. Her face looked red.

"I don't feel so good," she said.

I glanced back at the man but didn't see him anymore. So, I put an arm around Ella's shoulders.

"Come on," I said. "Let's get you out of here."

Chapter 5

·Getaway

I quickened my step as we walked down the hallway. There were plenty of people all around the ship to feel safe, but I sensed someone was watching us. Every time I turned a corner, I glanced behind, which was hard to do with Ella's arm draped over my neck.

When we finally reached Ella's, she reached into her purse and dropped her keys on the floor. I left her standing on her own to pick up the keys. She swayed backward. I swooped the keys up and caught her before she fell.

"Okay, here we go." I coaxed her to the door where I could slip the key inside the lock.

"Why are you helping me?"

"Why shouldn't I?" I said as I turned the lock.

"You're so nice—I hate it." The door clicked, and before I could turn the knob, Ella said in a small voice, "I was horrible, wasn't I?"

"What? No."

She put a finger to my lips. "Shh, don't tell me. I know I was. I am. I know I am. It's just so hard." She was slurring badly now. The more she slurred, the tighter she clung to me, and the deeper her nails dug into my shoulder.

"Ella," I tried interjecting as I opened the door, but she wouldn't stop rambling.

"I am proving myself to that horrible man, and I didn't even notice, I didn't even," she hiccuped.

"What man?" I asked, leading her inside and closing the door behind us. She couldn't have been talking about Ace, though I know she'd been interested in earning his perfection.

I set her down on the sofa and she looked up at me. "I am becoming just like him. Mom used to tell me that when she was alive, not often, but when I was bad, she'd say to me, '*Ella, you are just like your father*,'" she said with a Southern inflection. Then she sobbed. "And I am!" She fell into the cushions.

"Your father?" I repeated, but she was oblivious.

Heels Dug In

"I was nice once upon a time, wasn't I? When she was alive, we were friends, remember?" Ella pushed her hair out of her face so I could see her eyes shining. "When Mom died and I had to live with *him*, he said I had to prove myself. All of our family fortune and I could only have it if I proved myself. Stupid, stupid." She pressed her hand to her forehead. "I thought he meant school, beauty pageants, all the things we did, do you remember them?"

"I do," I said.

She nodded as if she heard me, but the way Ella rolled into the couch told me she was not entirely in her own body, let alone aware of me. She hugged a pillow. "He meant the Blue Diamond. I run it well. I make money for him. I make so much money—so much damn money, they all hate me."

She buried her head in the pillow.

"Ella?" I pushed her hair to the side gently.

Her mouth was open wide and a soft snore escaped. I couldn't help but chuckle. One single, simple laugh that would have offended her if she'd heard it. But I wasn't mocking her. I was laughing at myself and how wrong I could be about someone.

I shouldn't have given up on her in boarding school. Ella wasn't cold-hearted, money-driven, or uptight: she was heartbroken. Trying to win the approval of a tyrant she'd been stuck with since she was fourteen years old had made her into someone she was not.

I slid her heels off her feet, then tugged the comforter away from her bed and pulled it up to her shoulders. I still viewed her as competition for the man of my dreams, but that didn't stop me from hoping her dreams would come true one day—with another man. I tiptoed to the door, opened it, and slipped out of the room. Clicking the door shut, I turned to see a figure dart into the shadows.

My senses went on high alert. My heart raced as I began walking. I tried not to let it show that I'd seen something, but there was no ignoring the hair-raising alarm my brain was sending through my body.

Someone was following me.

Chapter 6

Tall, Dark Stranger

The hall was all-clear, except for a pair of tipsy honeymooners heading back to their room, rings on display as they held hands and clung to each other. Still, there were plenty of places to hide—side rooms, doorways, staircases, and so on. The architecture was ideal for leaping out of dark corners and kidnapping.

I turned on my heels and bolted back to the bar. Down the hallway and around the corner, I could see the singles dancing and chatting away with no cares in the world.

Once I was safely past the wide-open double doors, I slowed to a walk. My heart was racing as I looked behind me, but there was still no one there. I felt a little silly with my hot face and clammy hands. I put a hand on my neck, calming myself so that the sweat could dissipate.

Glancing around, I saw no sign of that stranger I'd noticed before. I took a deep breath and headed for the bar.

I needed something after a night like this, but it wouldn't be alcohol. A virgin hot toddy maybe; it would have to be something that would allow me to stay sharp.

If I were lucky, I'd catch a glimpse of whoever had been following me and make it back to my room to see if he matched the description of any suspect in the case files. I checked my watch: 11:00 p.m. Lafitte should be bringing the paperwork to the room any time now. And Ace should be back from whatever he'd done with his night.

What was he doing? I hadn't thought of that earlier. I was sure he was investigating, but who and where I had no idea. Looking around the bar, I wondered if he might have entered the Single Mingle area after all.

Beside me, the scent of a sea breeze cologne filled the air. In my periphery, I could see a man taking the seat next to mine. I turned, ready to give Ace a little teasing before making up for our half-pretend spat earlier.

But it wasn't Ace. It was that dark-haired stranger from earlier, leaning on his elbow at the bar. He smiled at me like a man who'd just won a game of cat and mouse. I crossed my arms, tapping my acrylic nails.

Heels Dug In

"You followed me, didn't you?"

"For your safety, I assure you," he said, reaching for something in his jacket pocket.

I stiffened, ready to deck him, run, or cry murder as necessary. He pulled out a badge. He was part of the ship's security—or he was pretending to be. He flashed the badge so fast I hadn't read the name.

"Did your friend make it inside safely?" he asked in a French accent. Mondragon International really was an international cruise line.

"Yes," I said, still skeptical of his intentions.

"I'm glad. She seemed upset."

"She's tough. She'll be fine."

"I'm relieved to hear it."

"So, other than stalking my friend, was there some other reason you were following us?"

He held his hands up. "I'm not stalking your friend— or you for that matter. My name is Pierre Lafitte, head of this ship's security. I believe you and your...husband...requested some information from me."

The way he said *"husband"* and how he phrased our investigation as a request for information made me wonder if Lizzy had told him our real identities. She'd said she didn't know who to trust. I took it that meant the crew and security officers, too. I kept my guard up—just in case.

"Lafitte?" I said. "Lizzy told us we'd meet you later."

"I made it earlier. Naturally, I've had a special concern regarding you two, knowing that you are friends with Miss Mondragon."

"Thank you, but I don't think we should get any special treatment," I said.

"Let me be clear. My concern is about you, not for you. Your spouse is under special watch since he was seen arguing just now with the captain."

Disappointment pulled at my lips. *Had he gone off to see Damian after we parted? Did he feel he had unfinished business that took precedence over our investigation?*

"What happened? Did he get hurt?" I asked.

"No, your husband is fine. Do you have a reason to believe he would get into a physical altercation with the captain?" he asked.

I knew the question was an accusation, but the excuse was an easy enough one to defend. "They are half-brothers."

Lafitte's face changed to surprise. "Brothers? C'est vrai? Is that true?" He put a hand to his chin. "Then, perhaps the motive was personal."

Heels Dug In

I narrowed my eyes. "Motive? For what? Was someone hurt?"

He leaned closer to me, as if sharing a secret. "I would not come right out and say this to just anyone, but since you are the captain's sister-in-law, I will tell you: there has been a murder in the captain's quarters."

"Oh no, is Damien—"

Lafitte put a hand up. "The captain is fine. It was a stowaway. He somehow snuck into the captain's quarters."

"Then it was self-defense? Damien would have been well within his rights to defend himself."

"I did not say the captain struck him, only that he died in his quarters."

"Surely, you don't suspect my...Ace?"

My inability to call Ace my husband would work against us. No one would believe I was married to Ace if I couldn't even say the word *husband* aloud. Of course, my sitting in a singles bar didn't do much to back up our story, either.

Lafitte smiled like a wolf.

"He is the captain's brother, so their argument could have been a natural one. Still, as I cannot find your husband, it does not look good. Perhaps if you can call him, we could clear things up?"

I took my phone from my purse and began to dial his cell. The ship's Wi-Fi was spotty, but I'd purchased cell service and Wi-Fi both to ensure a connection one way or the other—for both Ace and myself. It went through without a glitch.

As the phone rang, I said to Lafitte, "You know, you could've asked Damian. I'm sure he would've told you Ace was his brother."

"I did, but his answer, at the time, I did not understand."

"What was it?" I asked.

"He said, 'Someone I wish my father had never introduced to me.'"

Chapter 7

Lost at Sea

Lafitte and I discovered Ace had followed the suspicious couple to the crew quarters. He would have called ship's security soon if I hadn't called him. When we got to the hallway where Ace had been spying, he held up a hand for us to stop outside a room where the door was ajar.

"Wait," he said. "They're a harmless couple, but they're refusing to leave."

"What are they doing here? Stealing?" Lafitte asked, already drawing a gun.

"There's no need for that," Ace said.

Without hesitating, Lafitte pushed past Ace and walked into the open room. Ace and I exchanged a wide-eyed look as we heard him shouting for the couple to freeze. I joined Ace in the doorway.

Furniture lay scattered across every inch of the room. The Roberts stood with their hands up. Their expressions read angry and annoyed rather than guilty and afraid. Lafitte lowered the gun just enough for them to relax.

"This is not what it looks like, I can assure you," the man said in his thick accent.

"We can explain," the woman added. She spoke softly, more like a woman who should be knitting sweaters than one who was currently holding up one that belonged to a victim of her robbery.

"You can explain why you are in a crewman's quarters going through his things? Let me guess, not stealing?" Lafitte's tone dripped with sarcasm as he took out a walk-talkie and called for backup.

"I would never!" The man's hand curled into fists.

"We're only looking for clues," the woman said, sounding more like a church member than a thief.

"As you should've been doing." The man waved the crumpled t-shirt at Lafitte.

"What do you mean, looking for clues?" I stepped farther into the room.

"They're looking into the recent disappearances on this ship," Ace said.

Heels Dug In

"Four girls missing, and you are doing nothing about it," the man sneered.

Lafitte raised an eyebrow. "You are the investigators?" His tone was skeptical. Perhaps Lizzy hadn't told Lafitte our names. Now, he assumed it was this couple.

"Well, no, not exactly investigators," the woman replied.

The man threw the shirt down on the bed. "The last girl who was taken was Emily Roberts, our daughter." His voice cracked on the last word, and he looked up as if both pleading with some higher power and trying desperately not to cry.

The woman rested a hand on her husband's shoulder. Though her eyes were teary, her voice shook less. "We're Mary and Glenn Roberts. Emily went missing last month."

"You're the ones who—" I stopped. I couldn't outright say that they were the ones who had threatened to sue the Mondragon company. I rephrased my thought: "Your daughter was a crewmate, wasn't she?"

Mary nodded. Glenn wrapped an arm around his wife.

"This was her room. Much good it did her to be a member of this blasted company. They didn't protect her. They're not even looking for her."

Lafitte holstered his pistol. "I assure you we are taking the matter very seriously. I can appreciate your need for answers, and I can forgive this…misunderstanding. Still, you need to leave the matter with my security team and not go breaking into any more cabins."

Glenn straightened. "We won't stop searching for answers."

"You won't be able to search at all in the brig. I'm sorry, truly, for your predicament, but trespassing is a crime for which I am well within my authority to make an arrest." Lafitte walked behind the bed and ushered the couple out of the room.

Glenn and his wife moved along with him, but not without protest. Glenn said, "Arrest us if you want, but we'll have justice for our daughter."

That sounded a lot like revenge. Still, I couldn't see the Roberts as killers.

"I don't think an arrest is necessary. I can't imagine how you feel, but there are ways to search the ship without breaking the law. We can help you if you want," I offered.

Heels Dug In

"Who are you? You look familiar," Mary said.

I wasn't sure if Mary meant she'd remembered me from the shuttle to the boat or if she'd seen me in magazines from my previous career as a model. The way she looked at me, she might have seen me as a suspect.

"Kaitlynn Sa-East. Kait East. I'm just a passenger."

The man grunted. "You are very kind. You and your husband both. But I don't know if there's anything you can do. No one can help us, it seems."

"Mr. Roberts," I said. "Trust me, if there is anyone on this ship who can help you, it's us."

Chapter 8

Secret Romance

Ace and I woke early the next morning. I showered and dressed before him, opting for a low-key, knee-length, lavender, floral jumpsuit. I dried my hair in the room as Ace showered and prepared for the day. It was going to be a busy one: breakfast with the Roberts, a visit to the morgue with Lafitte, and dinner at the captain's table—if we could stomach it.

I curled my hair, texturized, and brushed it out like a pro. I flipped the last of the blonde waves behind my shoulder as Ace stepped out, ready for the day. I caught a glimpse of him staring, his eyes tracing my body from curls to curves as he entered the room. I smirked.

Look all you want.

He looked away, adjusting his collar he reached for his watch and wallet. I wrapped the cord on my curling iron and set it on the dresser to cool. In the mirror behind me, Ace snapped the watchband on his wrist. His navy pants and baby blush, short-sleeved button-down was at least less formal than yesterday's outfit. He'd opened three buttons on the collar, which was as easygoing as I'd seen Ace's attire. I knew this trip was about the missing girls, but I hoped I'd have an opportunity to buy a few choice pieces in the casual wear missing from Ace's closet.

That sea breeze cologne he wore sparked images of us picnicking on the beach—a perfect honeymoon scene. If only the rings around our fingers represented a real commitment.

Ace walked past me, opening the door.

"Ready?" he asked.

"As I'll ever be."

We left our room, heading straight for the breakfast bar. It was an outdoor area on deck with a view of the ocean and the on-deck swimming pool. Ace waved to Mr. and Mrs. Roberts, who were already seated, and we joined them with our breakfast orders soon enough. I was grateful for my latte and muffin, which was far more appetizing than Ace's black coffee and oatmeal. The Roberts were too distressed to eat anything, except for the complimentary croissants.

"We're not rich," Glenn divulged. "When we moved to the U.S., we had a flourishing mystery magazine. But we failed to change with the times when everything went online."

"We changed that. Now we're publishing mysteries and true crime in an online magazine, which includes exposing the Mondragons, if that's what it takes to find our daughter." Mrs. Roberts' voice broke. Her husband stroked her back, and she finished the last bite of her chocolate croissant and used her napkin to dry her eyes.

"I'm so sorry about what happened to Emily," I said.

"Anything you can tell us might help us find her," Ace said.

Glenn took out his wallet, his breath hitching as he took out a picture and handed it to Ace. Sitting next to Ace, I could see the image of a girl who looked younger than me.

In all of the prime-time stories I'd seen of missing or murdered women, the reporters used similar language. They described each victim as having "a smile that lit up the room" or being "full of life." Emily had that beaming smile. Her blue eyes shone in the flash of the camera with joyful energy.

Her father fought back tears. "Emily was only nineteen. She was so excited about traveling the world.

We didn't have the money for college, so she thought she'd travel and build up her savings so that she could get a degree in journalism."

"Journalism? She must've been inquisitive," I said.

"Too curious," her mother smiled. "She was always asking questions, noticing details. Once she had a question, she wouldn't let go until she had an answer."

"Did she notice anything strange on board?" Ace asked.

"Not that she said to us. She had a travel blog, which we read to keep updated. But it was all sand and sunshine. She had not a bad word for anyone," Glenn said.

"Not entirely true," Mary countered. "She had a romantic interest on board. A member of the ship's crew. She wouldn't tell us who he was—only that he didn't want to reveal it yet out of fear of one or both of them losing their jobs. Staff is not supposed to fraternize."

"Did she say anything else about him? Any hints about his identity?" Ace took his notebook out, jotting down the words *secret romance.*

Mary said, "Not a thing past him being a crewmate and her loving his accent. Only, every crewmate seems to have an accent of some kind—or almost everyone. You'd think the man in question would have admitted to his relationship with her."

"Unless he's got something to do with her going missing," Glenn said. "I wonder if she didn't break up with him. Men can go into a rage when they're rejected."

"Did they have an argument?"

Mary teared up. "She stopped communicating with us the last few days of the trip. Poor reception on the island is what we thought." She took out her smartphone, scrolling through it. Then, she handed the phone to me.

"This is the last picture she sent us."

It was a close-up of a seashell flower hairpin. In the background stood a dark-skinned man holding up a wreath with seashells on it. His mouth was open as if talking. From past experience, I assumed this was a vendor calling out prices to attract customers. It was a typical scene of a marketplace I'd been to before. After Ace had glanced at the phone, I handed it back.

"Was there anything else? Photos she hadn't sent yet or any unposted drafts on her blog?" I asked, hoping for any helpful information.

Mary shook her head. "The police officials took her phone and laptop, so we don't know what might've been on them."

Glenn puffed up his chest. "They'll be hearing an earful from us, too. If they don't help us find her, we'll have no recourse but to print about their cover-up of this crime."

"You think the local police are involved?" Ace asked.

Glenn tossed the crumpled napkin from his hands onto the table. "All I know is that these cases don't get solved on this island. Our daughter isn't the first to go missing, and if the police on the cruise and island are not willing to find them, more will disappear before this cruise is over."

"That will not happen." Lafitte appeared a few feet away, his thick accent turning a few heads. Lafitte smiled reassuringly to the girls at the next table, all of whom had worried looks on their faces. I realized that some of the nearby passengers had picked up on our conversation. Disturbed glances passed between eavesdroppers. The Roberts didn't seem to care, but Lafitte did not look pleased.

"On that topic, your background checks out, Mr. East. It seems that you are an investigator. How lucky for us that you were on board." He looked at Ace with an intense gaze. I had the feeling he could see through our cover, but we'd stayed true to Lizzy's promise not to tell him we were here specifically to investigate the disappearances.

Ace set down his napkin and stood. I followed. So did the Roberts. I doubted they knew about yesterday's murder. Lafitte would not have shared that with the already troubled parents. And the Mondragon cruise line would not want that publicity spreading aboard like wildfire. They must have thought they'd aid in our search for their daughter.

Lafitte held a palm toward them. "I am sorry, but this is an official ship investigation. I cannot allow you to follow."

"She's our daughter." Glenn's voice rose as if taking advantage of having an audience.

Ace placed a hand on his shoulder. "We'll keep you informed of any progress we make in this case. I promise."

This seemed to appease him, though he still gave Lafitte a suspicious eye and shared a glance with his wife.

"What do we do?" Mary asked.

"You could explore the ship—the areas available to the public—and try not to worry."

That felt so empty, and my stomach twisted to say it, but there was nothing else I could tell them, so I gave a sympathetic smile and turned away.

Lafitte led us past the pool and the sunbathers. I spotted Ella surrounded by two possible suitors, seeming to be engaged in polite conversation. *Good for her.* I grinned as I walked past, not expecting Ella to react to me.

She jumped out of her seat, calling, "Kait!" As she neared, she blinked, seeing Ace as if she hadn't noticed him before.

"Ella?" Ace asked. I hadn't mentioned seeing her yesterday. Still, I wasn't sure if he was stunned by her surprise appearance or the amount of skin revealed by her bikini.

"Ace, hi. Um, congratulations, I suppose, are in order."

I was glad to see that Ace had composed himself, but Ella blushed deeply. It was almost painful to watch the burn appear on her cheeks. I couldn't give her any hints as to Ace's and my true reasons for coming on the cruise. I didn't want her getting mixed up in our potentially dangerous investigation—or realizing Ace was not, in fact, taken. I put a hand on Ace's shoulder, formulating a polite response that also gave her the message to stay away.

Lafitte had other plans. He stepped forward, reaching out for Ella's hand. "Enchanté. May I say, Miss Belle, that you are bewitchingly beautiful."

Ella's face matched her red hair as he kissed her hand. She brought her other hand to her lips, not entirely covering her smile. Ace glanced at me. I gave a puzzled look back. Did his worried expression mean he found Lafitte's charm as alarming as I did, or was he jealous of the pass he was making on Ella?

Giggling, the Southern twang that betrayed her roots came back to Ella's voice. "It's a pleasure to meet you, too, Mister…"

"Lafitte. Pierre Lafitte is my name, mademoiselle."

"But how did you know mine?" Ella looked at me, not entirely displeased that I'd share her name with him, which I hadn't.

"As head of the ship's security, madam, I stay aware of any passengers who…stand out."

I had to end this before she looked like a patient in a third-degree burn ward. I stepped closer to them, acting like SPF. "We actually have some important business with Lafitte."

Ace finished my thought. "If you'll excuse us, Ella, we'll have to catch up with you another time."

Ella raised a brow, eyes narrowing. "You're working a case, aren't you? Are you here undercover?"

"Undercover?" Lafitte raised an eyebrow.

Heels Dug In

I should have known Ella would pick up on the truth. She might've been handed her position as manager of her father's mall, but she kept a mental filing of every store owner, every crunched number, and all the details a lesser manager might never notice. Of course she'd put together that we were here specifically to investigate. She might be on vacation, but her mind wasn't away for the weekend.

"Sorry. Can't share anything. Have fun sunbathing," I said as I pulled Ace away.

Lafitte dragged his feet, giving Ella an apologetic expression, the pain in his eyes really too much for a first meeting. I was beginning to think he'd followed us last night for different reasons than he admitted.

But at least he wasn't the man who had stood at the bar last night watching Ella with creepy eyes.

***

Ace and I finally arrived at our next destination. The morgue was dim and cold. The body on the table reeked, despite the cold storage. I put a hand to my nose and mouth. I'd seen two other unfortunate people lose their lives, but I'd never get used to it.

As we walked up to the table, I took small steps behind Ace as he moved boldly forward. I stopped as soon as I was close enough to see the face. Stone cold dead as he was, he froze me to my core. I recognized him from the bar where I'd met Ella yesterday.

This man was our stalker.

"Who was he?" I asked.

"Jamison Oliver," Lafitte answered. "That's what his ID says. He was a navy man who was kicked out for insubordination and assaulting an officer."

"Sounds charming," I said, while Ace took down the name on his notepad. "How did he die?"

"The cause of the death was pufferfish toxin. We found some in the remnants of a partially eaten meal in the captain's room, which is why we believe the captain was the target."

"I doubt the man broke into the captain's room to eat his fish," I said.

"Yet, the captain insists that's what happened."

"He says he didn't know the man?" Ace asked.

"He is not saying anything—only that he has a ship to run. But I can rule out the captain, Mr. East. Our ship's coroner has just confirmed that the death occurred at a time when the captain has an ironclad alibi."

"Arguing with me," Ace reasoned.

"Precisely," Lafitte said.

"Who else would have access to the captain's room?" I asked.

Heels Dug In

He shrugged. "The first mate, myself, cleaning crew. Cruise cabins are not like houses—they're accessible to many people."

I put a hand to my neck, rubbing the stress knot forming there. "You're saying it could be anyone."

Not just with Jamison Oliver's death, but with Emily and the other missing girls, I was beginning to think there was no way we'd catch the culprit. The sea was just too vast, and the ship was, as Lafitte said, not like home. But the *Fire on the Sea* was Lafitte's charge, and he steered the investigation in a different direction.

"We should not be asking who had access, we should be asking who had a motive."

"Any leads?" Ace asked.

"I will when I find out more about the victim. I've sent out requests for information from Oliver's commanding officers, and I have a man conducting a background check as we speak."

Ace tapped on his notepad. "In the meantime, we'll have to find out more about the people in charge. Where was the first mate?"

Lafitte shook his head. "Mr. Redmont was on the navigation deck. He could not have been involved."

Astoria Wright

I bit my tongue. I'd heard that before, but I'd learned in cases like these that the people who seem the least likely were often the ones who were guilty.

Chapter 9

Travel and Travesties

Ace stayed with Lafitte, going over old security files a second time with a fine-tooth comb. Meanwhile, I opted for action-based sleuthing, with Lafitte's officers following—or stalking—me as I did so. A typical passenger might not have noticed the two men trying to appear nonchalant or the wires curled around the men's ears. I, however, realized seconds after leaving the morgue that I was being tailed. I successfully lost them once or twice. It was long enough for me to explore the layout of the ship. My discoveries were three-fold.

Firstly, I learned the hard way that the second officer was a woman named Wendy Rackham. She gave the impression of a serious sailor who wouldn't hesitate to "throw me in the brig" if she saw me wandering near the navigation deck again. Secondly, I caught a glimpse of

Cory Redmont, the first mate, whom one of the security officers described as a moody man who changed with the weather. The officer painted the image of a vain man as deep as a puddle with a fake charm as vast as the ocean when it came to beautiful women. I'd met a man or two like that in the modeling world. And with his broad shoulders, blond hair, and dimples, he looked like he'd fit right in with that crowd.

My third discovery was that the main security officer, a man whom Lafitte had assigned to follow me "for my safety," was a man named Kaden Bowen. Bowen added to my list of suspects with accents, with his South African dialect. On an international cruise, an accent was not a helpful clue for identifying a person of interest in a disappearance. Emily's boyfriend could be any number of candidates, including Lafitte himself.

If the way he kept after Ella was a common routine for him, he might have had any number of female passengers or crew falling for his charms. Or his traps. But I had no reason to suspect him other than his foreignness and his flirting with Ella.

And his flirting had apparently continued long enough for him to ask Ella to dinner. Ace had apparently been there for the exchange. He told me as we prepared for our first formal dinner with the captain. I stepped out of the bathroom as Ace was putting on his jacket.

"So, it looks like Ella is joining us since Lafitte always dines with the—with Damian," Ace said.

"I thought the crew wasn't supposed to woo their guests."

Ace rolled the lint brush I'd brought over his sleeve. "People are human. Emily dated a crewmate. Rules are hard to follow when it comes to emotions."

I smirked as Ace set down the lint brush and picked up my necklace. He didn't realize his words could apply to us. I turned around, brushing my hair to the side as Ace draped the string of pearls around my neck. Once the clasp snapped closed, his hands reached for my hair, bringing the strands back into place. It was a small gesture that was unnecessary but meaningful.

Every time I began to wonder if he felt anything at all, he'd make those small gestures. Even if he didn't mean to, or if he'd chosen not to show his emotions, he still felt the way I did. But he was feeling something else, too, tonight. I saw the pensive look and the shadow of doubt reflected in his ash-gray eyes as we walked in the moonlight toward the dining hall.

"What's wrong?" I asked him.

"Damien."

It took me a second to realize he wasn't responding to me but greeting his brother. The captain neared the hall as we were passing the entryway. He stopped and held a hand out, gesturing for us to go ahead of him.

He greeted me with a nod and Ace with a formal, "Aeson."

They didn't seem to have moved past first names—except for whatever argument they'd had yesterday. The silent walk to the table in a room full of lively discussion left me grasping for words.

Ella found enough to fill the void. She and Lafitte were already at the table. Lafitte stood to greet us, and Ella complimented the captain as we sat down.

"The cruise has been amazing so far, Captain East." She flashed Ace and me a gotcha look, as if smug about figuring out that the captain was Ace's half-brother.

The captain tilted his head, looking at Ella, amused. "I don't believe we've met."

"Ella Belle," she said, holding out her hand. The captain took it like an old-fashioned gentleman, kissing the back of it. The last time I remembered seeing Ella blush like that was when she had fallen off a stage step in a pageant as a teen. That had been a mix of rage and embarrassment. This was a smile hidden with one hand

and darting eyes that didn't know where to look. She didn't know what to do with the compliment.

"Ella was kind enough to agree to be my date for this evening," Lafitte said.

"Then you are a lucky man," Damian replied, eyes glued to Ella. Then, pausing, he turned his gaze to me. "And so is my brother."

"Thank you. Is there some equally lucky woman in your life, Captain East?"

"You can call me Damian. And, no. I haven't found the right person yet."

The waiter came around with the menus. Damian took one, thanked the waiter, and focused his attention on the selections. While Ella kept the waiter occupied with questions and Lafitte attempted to guide her on the best dinner choices, Ace watched Damian intently.

"Why not order the swordfish?" Ace asked.

Damian lifted his eyes from the menu to stare at Ace.

Ella, thinking he'd spoken to her, said, "That's a good one. Or, how about this?" She pointed to something on the menu.

"Maybe not the pufferfish," Lafitte advised.

Then he paused. So did Ella. They had finally noticed the staring contest going on between half-brothers. I knew Ace was silently challenging Damian, but what swordfish had to do with it I couldn't understand.

"You didn't order pufferfish the other night, did you?" Ace asked.

Ella looked at me, questioningly. She didn't know about the murder, and I wasn't going to tell her. I remembered my promise to Lizzy. But Ella was sharp enough to figure out that something was wrong.

"Are you allergic to fish or something?" she asked.

Ace looked at her. "His mother was, and he inherited it from her. It's what kept you from joining the navy with your friend Jamison Oliver, isn't it?"

Damian set the menu down. "Is that what you and Lafitte found out in your investigation?"

Ella glanced back and forth between Ace and Damian, clearly picking up events based on context. She was too engrossed in their back-and-forth exchange to ask any questions. I glared at Lafitte, hoping he'd pick up on my annoyance that he'd invited her into this situation.

"It's what you admitted to just now."

Damian smiled. "I forgot, you're a first-rate PI who I'm sure has investigated my family before. But you're not quite good enough. I'm not allergic to fish. If I were, I'd have alerted the chef to the allergy, and you can ask him: he'll tell you I've never made any such request."

"But, you do avoid fish." Lafitte's expression was skeptical. "Now that I think about it, I have never seen you eat it."

"I have eaten seafood on occasion, Lafitte; I just don't prefer it. I had one incident in my childhood with a mild reaction and nothing since then. Whatever allergy I might have had, I outgrew it."

"Was that before or after you met Jamison?" Ace said.

Damian looked at the waiter, who seemed to have forgotten he was taking drink orders. The waiter looked at me.

Realizing I hadn't ordered, I said, "Just water, thanks."

"Yeah, same, fine," Ella said without looking at the man.

Damian watched the waiter go, glanced around the room, then spoke.

"Okay, yes. I knew Jamison."

"You were harboring a criminal."

"Criminal?"

"A disgracefully discharged naval officer who stowed away on this ship," Lafitte clarified.

"Disgracefully discharged." Damian shook his head. "Let me tell you about the officer you call a criminal. He saw a lieutenant commander harassing a female ensign and came to her aid. The violence began on the commanding officer's part—Jamison had a right to defend himself. If anyone should have been court-martialed, it was his C.O."

Ace had no response.

"Why did he have to stow away? Why not just pay for a ticket?" I said.

"I didn't realize I'd need a lawyer for this dinner." Damian picked up the menu.

"Afraid to answer the question?" Ace said.

"The answer will come out eventually. Tonight, will you please just try to enjoy the dinner?"

And that was all he said on the topic the rest of the night. Damian wasn't unpleasant. He certainly kept up a livelier conversation than Ace, since he sat silently through most of the meal. When the dinner was finally over, Damian excused himself, and Ella leaned forward toward me.

"What's with Ace, did someone die?"

"What makes you say that?" I knew the second the words flew out of my mouth that I showed too much alarm.

Ella jumped back. "Nothing, it's an expression." She leaned toward me again. "You and Ace are here on a case, aren't you? Someone really did die, didn't they?"

Heels Dug In

I couldn't answer her question honestly without her wanting to hear the whole truth. And I couldn't lie and expect her to just accept it. I stuck with a half-truth.

"Someone had a reaction to the pufferfish—we're just helping Lafitte out."

"You think the captain was involved in the murder?"

"No," I said. "We don't know for sure if it was murder or an accident."

But Ace, who'd heard us, said, "Yes." He caught the sharp look I was giving him and relented. "All right, no, we're not 100 percent sure about anything yet."

"We are still investigating," Lafitte added.

"And we're just helping," I said.

Ella raised an eyebrow. "And you're not undercover, secretly posing—" She caught herself, perhaps not wanting to blow our cover. "Never mind. I won't pry about that. But I want in on the case."

"Pardon?" Lafitte asked.

"I can help. I have helped before."

"It could be dangerous," I said.

Ella scooted closer to Lafitte. "That's why I have you to protect me." She looked between all three of our skeptical faces. "Come on, it's been years since I had a vacation. I don't know what to do with myself. My brain isn't used to not worrying about something. I'd like to help."

"Look, if there's anything you can do, we'll let you know. Otherwise, just stay out of it," I said.

Ella's nostrils flared and her eyes widened. Oh no, I'd pressed a button.

Ella didn't wait to finish dessert before standing up and saying, "Thank you, Pierre. It was a lovely meal."

Pierre rose from his seat. "Mademoiselle, are you done for the evening?"

"Oh, yes, I'm done." She looked at me. "You know, Kait, I'm not so blind that I can't see what's going on here. Lizzy asked me about you, and here you are. I know that's not a coincidence. I might not be the best friend ever of you and all your cliques from school, but I thought we were finally past our high school drama. I guess some people never change."

I blinked as she and Lafitte walked away. Somewhere in my mind, I registered Ace's hand on my shoulder and the words "Are you okay?" but I couldn't answer.

I knew Ella was being melodramatic. She always had a flair for that in school. But did she really think that I had excluded her from my "cliques?" I didn't control my friends, and I never kept Ella out of anything—not on purpose. She was the one who'd acted like school competitions were everything. She was the one who criticized and judged and had to be the best, bar none. But then, she'd had her reasons for that, as she'd explained last night. Had I misunderstood her this whole time?

"You know, it might not be bad to bring Ella in on this case," Ace suggested.

I looked at him, incredulous. "You want to put her in danger?"

"No, but I don't want you in any either. You split up to wander the ship yourself today. It might've been good to have someone with you."

"I did. Lafitte's men followed me." He didn't bat an eye. I crossed my arms. "But, of course, you knew that. Were you the one who suggested it?"

He sighed. "I just want you to be safe."

I relaxed my defensive stance, but not my position on the topic. "Putting Ella in danger isn't going to make me safer. Besides, the real danger is on the island, according to Lizzy. So, let's just get a good night's sleep and be on our guard tomorrow."

I stood up. Ace did the same, saying, "You're right. Tomorrow the real investigation begins on the island— and I have a bad feeling about it."

Chapter 10

Port of Call

Sand, sky, and sea—it had been so long since I'd been on a beach that I'd almost forgotten how the scenery could erase my cares. As we traveled to the beachside resort, I could picture Ace and myself sitting at any one of the cantinas or restaurants, looking out at the ocean while sharing a romantic meal.

Then I remembered the look on the Roberts' faces when they'd told us about their daughter, and my moment of reprieve ended. We were here to catch kidnappers—and possibly murderers. I shuddered at the thought. Ace noticed my shiver and began pulling his charcoal suit jacket off. I held a hand up to stop him.

I didn't explain that worry, not the breeze coming off the ocean, had caused my sudden chill. I had to show him that I was as much a detective as he, and that meant not complaining that this case rattled my nerves.

The resort did wonders to ease anxiety. Minutes from shore, it stood guard over the beach like a seven-story sentinel. Built like a palace, the structure was a Tuscan style with an open courtyard at its center.

On the highest level, there sat a helicopter Lizzy must have used to fly in. I marveled at that kind of lifestyle but didn't think it was worth the constant nervous tension Lizzy seemed to feel—or the guards surrounding her wherever she traveled.

As soon as we checked in with the front desk, the hotel manager accompanied us to the special elevator that led to Lizzy's penthouse. He inserted the key into the slot and pushed the button. The glass doors closed, and we watched as the view of the pristine pool was replaced by the identically decorated arched hallways of each story. At the top, the halls were painted with 3D murals of underwater life and coral reefs.

I wasn't surprised to see that Lizzy's penthouse was furnished with what appeared to be high-end furniture. The suite spanned a third of the entire level, the other two suites reserved for those who could afford the luxury of uber-wealthy living—or those whom Lizzy had personally invited to stay. I had no doubt the offer would be open to Ace and me. Still, we'd chosen to remain on board overnight.

Lizzy was just the same as I remembered her. Sharply dressed, hair neatly styled, and wearing a business suit rather than our old school uniform, she sat with perfect posture. Her personal assistant, a woman in a gray pin-striped suit, showed us to the sofa across from Lizzy's chair. There was an open sofa chair beside Ace, but the assistant stood at Lizzy's side. An assortment of sweets and coffee sat at the table, which a maid offered to pour. I declined, and Ace poured his own into the empty cup.

Lizzy smiled, amused, and waved the maid away. Then she said, "Thank you both for coming."

"We're happy to help," I said.

Ace, too bluntly, said, "We would have been more helpful if we'd had the files of the missing girls for reference."

Lizzy nodded to her assistant. The woman in gray handed a stack of four manila envelopes to Ace. Setting down his tea, he gave two of the files to me. Of the two in his hands, Ace opened the first. Lizzy bent her head to see which one he had.

"Jenna Rose Argamy," she said. "She was the first one to go missing. Seventeen years old. She was last seen at dinner with her nineteen-year-old sister and her sister's boyfriend. We suspected the boyfriend at first, but he was cleared and went back to the U.S."

"What made you suspect the boyfriend?" I asked, glancing between Lizzy and the file.

"They had differing accounts of events. They opted to stay overnight in two hotel rooms instead of sleeping on the ship. The sister said she didn't see Jenna after dinner the night they arrived on the island. The sister's boyfriend said he spotted her the next morning, at the SeaCenter marketplace. It was determined from various eyewitness accounts that Jenna was, in fact, taken in the morning, so his account appears to be correct. The police came to believe Jenna had skipped breakfast to make a quick purchase at the shops before the ship's departure and was taken sometime before or after the purchase."

I opened the next file. Reading the following name, I asked, "What about Enaria Torrez?"

"We don't know much about her. She was in her twenties, traveling solo as part of the Single Mingle cruise, so she had no one who knew her personally to realize she was gone. Initially, we believed she fell overboard just before departure since there was no trace of her on the island, and no one remembered her leaving."

"What changed your mind?" I asked.

"Her purse. It wasn't on the ship. Some of the others said she'd talked about going to visit the shops on the island the next day. Maybe she did. Or perhaps she didn't get the chance."

"It's a similar story with this other file," Ace said, holding up the second of his two cases. He read, "Gia Kaden, age twenty-one, seen celebrating her birthday on the ship the night before, goes missing after announcing plans to go scuba diving." He closed the file. "She never made it to the scuba center."

Lizzy nodded. Her hands curled into fists. "The worst one is Emily. She was a member of the crew."

"We met her parents," I said.

Lizzy's eyes widened and a gasp escaped her lips. "They were on the cruise?"

"They want answers," I said.

Lizzy put a shaky hand to her forehead. Her assistant quickly poured her a glass of water. She took it with a smile that might have been as much to reassure herself as to thank the woman in gray. When she'd recovered, she said, "You might already know then, about Emily's disappearance?"

Ace and I looked at each other. "Not everything," I said.

Heels Dug In

"Why don't you tell us?" Ace encouraged, pointing at the file I had yet to look at in my hands.

I opened it to see Emily's radiant brown eyes staring back at me. The women in the pictures were all so different. One was a blonde, another had black hair, another a blue streak on blonde. Each was a different ethnicity, but they were all beautiful, young women, stolen for reasons I felt sick to imagine. Emily's eyes, so vibrant and happy, bore into mine as if saying: I had a promising life: love, family, hope, a future. I want it all back. Find me.

We couldn't let her down.

"Emily might be the key to solving this case. She kept a diary on her phone—the local police aren't sharing it all with us. Something in it pointed to a member of the Mondragon staff. She'd come to have her suspicions about the staff and shared with a confidant that she believed she knew where the girls had been taken," Lizzy explained.

"Who was the confidant?" I asked, weighing whether the mysterious boyfriend seemed more likely as the confidant or the corrupt staff member.

Ace asked, "Where?" He took out his notebook to jot down the suspected location of the girls' captivity.

Lizzy answered me first. "We don't know who she confided in, nor who she suspected. The person remained anonymous when they contacted the police." She turned to Ace. "The only problem is a report from a local. A woman was seen trying to run from two guys near the construction site for our water park, the Surfing Dragon. We do background checks on all of our workers, but things slip through the cracks sometimes." I didn't see the look on Ace's face, but Lizzy gave a defensive frown, saying, "We're not involved with the kidnappings. I'm here to make sure that none of our workers are involved. We're doing extensive reviews of the workers at the resort and on the construction site. I intend to cooperate fully with police."

"We don't question that," I said, flashing Ace a look.

I'd learned to be less emotionally involved in cases involving my friends. Still, I doubted Lizzy would call us into a case of kidnappings if she were the mastermind behind them. Even if the suspicion was against her company, I had a feeling it was someone directly involved on the ship. As she said, as much as she might have vetted her workers, mistakes could be made. And as horrible as they could be, mistakes were human.

"Is the Fire on the Sea the only vessel with disappearances happening?"

Heels Dug In

"The only one in our company," Lizzy said. "But I will decommission the cruise ship if it means saving lives."

I knew she meant it. It would mean losing the millions of dollars I was sure the ship made for them each year, but I was glad to see that she put lives ahead of dollars.

"I knew it." A voice came from the doorway. Ella entered, arms folded. She was followed by Lafitte and a confused-looking manager.

"I'm sorry, Miss, she had an invitation from you. I told her it was for later and did not include a plus one." The manager looked at Lafitte out of the corner of his eye.

Lafitte dipped his head respectfully toward Lizzy. "Given what we heard, I am glad I insisted on seeing Miss Belle safely here."

Lizzy put a hand up and the manager nodded, awkwardly turning around. As he headed back to the exit, Ella hurried into the room. Her bright pineapple romper did not match her dead-serious expression.

I couldn't believe she'd barge in here—with Lafitte, no less. On second thought, knowing her personality, I should have expected it. I closed Emily's file.

"Were you eavesdropping this whole time?" I asked.

"I was invited," Ella said.

"For dinner," Lizzy corrected.

"So, I'm a little early." Ella sat down on the sofa chair next to Ace. "You know, I'm only here because you weren't honest with me from the start." She stared Lizzy down.

Eyes wide, Lizzy asked, "What?"

"You called me to make small talk and sneak in a question about Ace and Kait. You never said that there were disappearances on your cruises or that you were under investigation. If I'd known that, I wouldn't have taken a cruise, which, by the way, you practically told me to do."

"When did I do that?"

In a mock snooty tone, Ella said, "'Oh, yes, our cruises are doing wonderfully, eight years running and five different vessels.'" Ella grimaced. "Remember when I said, 'I'll have to take one sometime,' and instead of telling me anything about the disappearances, you said, 'You absolutely should,' followed by an 'I've got to go.'"

"I didn't think you meant you'd take one right away."

Ella threw her hands up. "Why didn't you just tell me? You know I don't share secrets."

I thought back on incidents that disproved that and then realized that there weren't any. Ella could be a vindictive gossip once a friendship broke up, but, while we were friends, she hadn't betrayed a word said in confidence.

I sighed. "Well, you know now." I glanced sidelong at Ace, adding, "And if you really want to help on the case, like you said you did yesterday, there is a way you can."

"How?" Ella asked.

"There are two places to investigate, aren't there?" I said.

Ace collected the files. "All the girls had the marketplace in common. And the construction site has probably been combed over by police, but I can at least talk to some of the workers."

"I can go with you," Lafitte offered.

"Agreed. Ella and I can take the marketplace and see if there's anything suspicious there we can find," I said.

Lafitte turned to Ace, completely ignoring Ella and me as he said, "Maybe I should accompany the ladies. They should not go alone, right?"

Rolling my eyes, I said, "If you're so worried, you can send your team to follow us, but you might need them yourself if you're snooping around the area where they're keeping those girls." I stood up.

"Wait," Ace said. "At least take this." Ace took a small device out of his wallet and handed it to Ella. It was the tracker. Before I could argue that I had mine and he should keep one on him, too, he held a hand up. "Lafitte will be with me, and he's got walkie-talkies and a large team."

Lafitte agreed. "We will take some of my men with us, and some will go with you. Would that be all right?" He directed the question to Lizzy, whom I'd almost forgotten was his boss.

She nodded. "Keep a close eye on them. If they are harmed in any way, I'll hold you personally responsible."

Chapter 11

Hit the Town

Ella didn't seem to realize the danger investigating posed. She walked ahead of me to the road with the covered shops. The marketplace was buzzing with excitement. Ella went straight for the sunglasses. She picked a dark pair too large for her face.

"Ella, what are you doing?" I crossed my arms.

"Everyone's wearing them. If I'm going to be spying, I'm going to need to blend in." She opened her purse and paid the seller.

Between the shouts of the local salespeople calling out deals and specials, Ella and I heard the call of a merchant: *"Seashell flower pendants, only ten U.S. dollars!"*

We stared at each other. Ella slid her ridiculous shades to the tip of her nose. "Did he say...?"

Without a word, I walked briskly in the direction of the merchant's call. I heard Ella behind me.

"Where's it coming from?" she asked.

"I don't know."

I didn't know where he was, whether he was involved, or if this marketplace was the last place Emily and the other girls had gone. I knew that Lafitte's security team was nearby. Still, I felt this idea of us as bait was a bad one as we approached the shop where the seashell flowers were on display.

"Is this the right place?" Ella whispered.

I nodded. From what I remembered of Emily's picture, she had been here before.

The vendor closed in on us. Holding out a seashell flower necklace, he said, "Are you interested? Only ten dollars."

"Looks more like five to me," Ella retorted.

I gave her a disapproving glance. Bargaining might come naturally to her, but this was not the time—even if it was the right place.

I took out the picture from my bag. "Was this woman here three weeks ago? Does she look familiar?"

He lowered the necklace and peered at the picture. Then he pulled back, waving a palm at me.

"I'm not involved."

Heels Dug In

"Involved in what?" Ella asked.

"I believe you. All I want is some information. Did you see what happened to her?" I asked.

"No. I'm not involved."

His eyes shifted behind us, and I could tell he was spooked by the security men he saw there. He hooked the necklace back on a metal post attached to his booth. Then he shooed us away from his shop.

"What about the necklace?" Ella asked. She wasn't going to buy it; she just loved to make jabs.

"They're not for sale anymore. Go away," the man said.

I led Ella away, and we headed out of the marketplace. I glanced behind me several times, both happy and unnerved by the security still nonchalantly covering our trail. I wondered how Lizzy did this all the time. I had barely spent twenty minutes being tailed and already I was sick of it. I needed some air.

"Come on, we're not going to find anything here," I said as I headed for the last row toward the beach.

"That was a bust," Ella agreed. "Where to next?"

"Back to the resort, and before you argue, it *was* on the list," I said.

I knew Ella would insist on not being left out of the investigation, but the fact was that it was dangerous and friend, frenemy, or whatever I thought of Ella, I wanted her to be safe. Knowing her, she'd get caught up in the luxury of the place and lose track of time eventually anyway. Then I'd be free to join Ace for the real investigation.

I wondered if he'd found the contact Lizzy had mentioned yet, and if he'd discovered any clues about their whereabouts.

When we rounded the corner out of the marketplace, there were only a few seconds that passed before I spotted the answer to how the kidnappings were taking place.

I said to Ella, "One of the girls, Gia, said she wanted to go scuba diving but disappeared before she could get to the center."

"Okay, what does that mean?"

"Look." I pointed down the hill toward a small building with a couple of aging huts alongside it.

"Is that the scuba gear rental center?" Ella asked. "So, she must have been kidnapped between here and there."

I shook my head. "That's not the rental center—the center is a mile away according to the directory the ship gave us. There's no way this is the same one."

Ella shrugged. "So, it's something else."

Heels Dug In

"It says ferry service if you look carefully enough, but what if Gia mistook it for the center? What if all the girls, for whatever reasons, took this shortcut off the main path? We thought the construction site was a dangerous place, but past the marketplace, these older buildings look like they're being shut down or foreclosed. Even if the ferry service isn't directly involved, surrounded by abandoned buildings like it is, it's a prime spot for kidnapping."

"Then the kidnappers might be nearby," Ella said.

I nodded and looked down the dirt path. It looked like a shortcut directly from the marketplace to the rental building, and Ella and I began walking down—not far, just for a closer look. A few paces in, I slid on a rock. Thankful I was wearing a SensationSoles original pair of sneakers and not my usual heels, I shifted my center of gravity so I didn't fall. But I'd stumbled ahead of Ella, who, thankfully, wasn't laughing. Now that I saw that the route was steep and rocky, I realized this was a dangerous shortcut to take. The fact that there were several areas not visible from the top of the hill made me even more convinced that this was where the girls had been abducted.

"Let's wait for Lafitte's men," I said.

But Ella didn't respond.

Astoria Wright

I turned around to see Lafitte's security coming toward me, but they weren't coming to help us....

Chapter 12
Tourist Trap

The last thing I remembered was using the little Krav Maga Victoria had taught me to land a blow in my attacker's face. Ella and I had run the moment Lafitte's men tried to grab us. We dashed as fast as we could down the path. In retrospect that was a mistake, because the men from the ferry service cornered us, leaving me no choice but to try to land a well-aimed blow and make my way back up the hill. The next thing I knew, I was coming to in the dark with a pounding headache.

Ella's frantic breathing tickled my eardrum in the small space of what must have been a car trunk. She banged on the lid, repeating, "I'm not gonna die" like a mantra. I was surprised that neither her mouth nor mine had been taped, but our hands were tied. If they hadn't been, I might have strangled Ella myself.

"Will you please calm down? We have a limited air supply in here." I hissed, already feeling ill from the cramped space as we were driven to who-knows-where.

"Kait? Thank god. I thought you were dead."

I moved, crying out when pain jabbed at my temple. "Obviously, I'm alive. Where are we?"

"In a car that was parked at the bottom of the road. The ferry service was in on it, Kait. A guy came out of the shop and helped them put us in the trunk."

"Yeah, I was still awake for that. I meant, where are we on the road? Did we make any turns? Are we still facing west? How long have we been traveling?"

"I don't know, not long. Five minutes, maybe. No, I don't think we turned. We're in a trunk if you haven't noticed. It's not like I can see the road." She paused, then said, "You were amazing. I think you broke that guy's nose."

"That guy" was Kaden Bowen, the security officer. But he wasn't the one in charge. His commanding officer was Pierre Lafitte, whom I was now convinced was the man with the accent Emily had been dating.

"Lafitte betrayed us," I said.

"You don't know that."

Heels Dug In

If Ella could have seen me, I would have rolled my eyes. Love wasn't just blind. In her case, it was unable to process reality.

"He set us up, Ella. How else did they know you had a tracker?"

Silence. Ella couldn't answer that one. The men had taken the tracker out of Ella's purse and demanded mine. Instead of complying, I'd decked the man. I heard Ella scream before he'd decked me.

"I'm sorry," Ella said. "They found the tracker in your hair clip. There's no way for Ace to track us now."

I twisted, taking a mental note of what I still had on me. I hoped they hadn't found everything that I'd hidden on my body. They'd taken the purse, which included my phone. But they hadn't found the second one.

Ella began banging on the trunk lid again.

"Will you please stop that?" I asked. Every hit increased the pounding in my temples.

"At least I'm trying to get out. I don't want to be in here when they open the trunk."

"You don't want them opening the trunk because you're banging on it."

Ella stilled. After a stretch of silence, she said, "Sorry." Another second of silence passed, and she said, "God, Kait, are we going to die?"

"No," I said flatly, wishing I could ensure that my answer was true.

"What are we going to do?" Ella whimpered, sounding like she was going to start sobbing any second.

"We're not going to panic. And we're going to call for help."

"How? They took our cell phones and my tracker."

"I still have mine," I said.

'They took your purse. I saw them take out your phone."

"I still have a mini cell phone on me."

That was an understatement, it was the world's smallest cell phone—pricey, but worth every penny.

"Then what are you waiting for? Call for help."

"There's one problem: it's in my bra."

Ella paused. "You're telling me this why?"

I scowled even though she couldn't see me. It was as unpleasant a notion for me as it was for her, and I wasn't going to say it out loud. So I stuck with a simple command.

"You know why. Move."

"Ugh, fine." She shuffled over me. I shifted myself so that I was facing her. Turning so that her hands were facing my body, Ella reached back.

"Eww," she squealed as she touched skin.

"That's my chin," I said.

"Oh." She sounded relieved. "Okay, hold on. Which side?"

"Left."

"Really? Is that one bigger, because you always seemed a little lopsided to me."

I stopped myself from arguing against her completely unfounded accusation and focused. "It's in a side compartment with a zipper. If you're careful, you won't have to touch anything. Be careful."

I slid farther in her direction. She stifled a whine as she reached into my jumpsuit. Her fingers slid quickly to my side and I heard her sigh of relief as she found the zipper pocket. She had the cell phone out in seconds.

As the phone slid out of my collar, the screen lit.

"Sorry," Ella said. "Didn't mean to turn anything on."

I ignored the innuendo. "No, that's good. I can see the screen. Hold it there."

The mini cell phone was the old-fashioned design with actual buttons one could feel with their fingertips. There was no AI, but at least Ella might be able to dial by feel. I'd programmed Ace's number into my speed dial.

"Okay, you can feel the buttons. Press the star and number one. That will call Ace."

"What if the call doesn't go through? Service on the island is spotty."

I rolled my eyes. "If you don't try, we definitely won't be saved. Just dial."

"Fine." She pressed the buttons.

The phone rang once. Then twice. Come on, Ace, you know the plan. I silently prayed that he had already been tracking us. The click of his phone picking up sent a rush down my spine.

"Kait?" He sounded panicked.

"It's me," I answered.

"Thank god. I thought...the cliffs."

"They tossed our trackers."

"And Ella?"

Did he sound as worried about her as he was for me? I shook my head. Why shouldn't he be? Ella had put her life in danger as willingly as I had, and Ace and I were responsible for that.

"We're both fine, but we might not be for long. We're locked in a trunk. It's a black car, but I only caught a glimpse of it. I didn't get the make or model."

"I did. It's a two-door, black Honda civic," Ella chimed in.

"Any idea where you are?" Ace asked.

"Going down the coast heading west, I think."

Heels Dug In

"A black Honda civic by the shoreline. All right. I'll alert the police, and Lafitte and I will try to find you."

"No!" Ella and I responded at once.

"You can't trust Lafitte. He's the ringleader. It was his men who attacked us," I explained.

"You're sure? He was with me when I called in my tip to the police. He's with an officer of the British navy now, explaining what we found out here by the construction site."

"You found the girls?"

"Not exactly, but we have a lead. There used to be a ferry service on a rocky cove on the other side of the island. It's dangerous for boats to dock there, so it officially closed as a port decades ago. When we went to check it out, we saw a ferry coming into shore. We think they might be transporting the girls to the next island via ferry here. The Mondragon workers didn't need to be in on it, just the noise and confusion of a construction site provided enough cover."

"That makes sense. There's a ferry service by the marketplace."

"The ferry service was in on it," Ella said.

Ignoring her, I said, "If I'm right, we should be about twenty minutes away."

"We are?" Ella asked.

I could tell by the direction the car had been parked. Even though I'd only seen it for a second, it was parked facing away from the marketplace. We hadn't made any U-turns, and for the most part, our journey had been straight, veering only to the left, which would take us closer to shore. I didn't explain this to Ella. But, I was sure we'd be detouring once they saw the police cars and British naval officers. If they didn't get caught before they rerouted, they might get away with us in the trunk.

Twenty minutes to get rescued or we'd be lost forever. And I wasn't 100 percent sure about the destination. If I was wrong, Ella and I didn't have a chance.

"Try to hang in there. I'll have the police ready here, and I'll search the road personally." Ace was speaking in a low voice, perhaps so Lafitte couldn't hear.

"No, Ace. I have another idea. Call Lizzy. She's just about the only person who can search for us by air."

"Brilliant," Ace said. "I'll have her send her helicopter. Kait, don't worry. We will find you."

Chapter 13
Mai Tais and Alibis

After the worst twenty minutes of my life, I heard the swinging blades and shifting air of a helicopter.

"We're saved!" Ella squealed.

"Not yet," I said.

There were muffled sounds of distant yelling. The car lurched forward. Ella and I slammed against the back of the trunk. A high-speed chase was not what I'd hoped would result.

Ella started shouting, "I knew I shouldn't have helped you. I thought it would be like last time—how you and I helped catch that killer—this is so not like that. I'm going to die in a car chase, and it's all your fault!"

"Shh—"

"Don't shush me!"

"Ella, stop. Do you hear that?"

She began to argue, then she gasped as the sound of sirens blared ahead of us. The driver slammed on the brakes and it was all I could do to keep my head from smacking into the back of the trunk. Ella crashed forward and knocked the wind out of me.

But when the car skid to a halt, my breath returned.

"Get out of the car!" I heard in English. Several other commands were given in another language.

My heart pounding drowned out the other sounds, or maybe the men had given up. I could hear footsteps approaching. There had been no gunshots fired.

"Ella, I think we're saved."

"Mmm?" she said groggily.

"Ella? Are you hurt?" I asked.

"No, maybe." She sounded disoriented.

The trunk clicked open. An officer, dressed in a British naval uniform, reached out his hand and pulled me out of the trunk. Ace shouted somewhere in the distance. He appeared by my side in what seemed like seconds. Once I was standing, the officer reached in for Ella.

"I think she hit her head," I said, as Ace untied the zip ties around my wrists.

"I'm fine," Ella insisted. She put a hand to her head once her wrists were free. "It's not anything worse than yours." Even with injuries, she had to be competitive. I smiled and reached an arm around her. It was the first embrace in over a decade that I had shared with my old friend. She patted my shoulder.

"All right, yes, I'm glad you're alive too." She pretended she didn't care, but she was all smiles as we pulled away.

Lizzy walked toward us. Propriety forbade a hug, but she was beaming. She reached out to shake hands with Ace. He accepted the gesture.

"British navy officers are searching for the girls on the nearby island. We have reason to believe they're alive."

"And Lafitte?" Ace asked.

"The men captured are not admitting his involvement. One denies Lafitte knew anything at all. The police are taking him in for questioning anyway, but as long as there's nothing to tie him to this, I can only temporarily relieve him of duty during the investigation."

"So, he might not be involved?" Ella asked. I wished she didn't have that note of desperation in her tone. It was beneath her.

Lizzy couldn't give her a definite answer. Instead, she walked us back to her helicopter. We could easily have driven back with the officers, or with Lizzy's drivers, but the air-lift vehicle needed to be returned to the rooftop of the Mondragon resort anyway.

"We'll get a doctor for you both and a private jet home, for all of you," she reassured.

"Are you grounding the ship?"

"We're not sure yet, but it isn't scheduled to leave until tomorrow morning. The jet could be ready for you tomorrow morning."

"No, thank you," Ace and I said almost at once.

I smiled, glad that we were on the same page. "We'd like to return to the ship if that's all right. We don't feel we've done our job as long as the head of the operation is still at large."

"If the culprit is a member of the *Fire on the Sea* crew, we may be able to catch the criminal," Ace said.

"I just want to get my money's worth of my vacation. I'll leave the investigating to the two of you," Ella said.

Lizzy let out a laugh at Ella's comment. "I'm happy to issue you a refund. And Kait and Ace, I'm happy to have you working the case. I hope it's not someone on my cruise line behind everything, but if it is, I have every confidence you'll catch them."

Chapter 14

Traveler Check

The rough seas were hard on my stomach. I almost wished we'd stayed overnight at Lizzy's, but it was important to be back on board tonight. Every opportunity to investigate had to be taken. But at the moment, I needed some time to recover. I didn't need the Roberts coming up to me while Ace was off getting me a drink.

"Have you found anything?" Mr. Roberts asked.

"The British navy and local police are following a lead right now," I said.

"But is she alive?" Mrs. Roberts asked.

"They think so, but I don't know for certain."

Mrs. Roberts sobbed.

"We're still working on it," I assured. "As soon as we find out anything, we'll let you know."

Mr. Roberts put his arms around his wife. "We're on deck two, room 2201. You call the second you find out anything," he said.

I watched them walk away, rubbing my temples. I still had a headache from earlier, and the partying passengers in the limbo competition were making a ruckus that only added to it. The ground felt like it was moving beneath me. But it was the idea of a criminal mastermind on board that really made me queasy.

I gripped the railing as children raced by and swimmers dove into the pool. A luau celebration onboard, an excuse for showing off bikini bodies, meant a hundred carefree cruise passengers who were blissfully unaware of what had transpired on this trip. Back home, they might turn on their TVs and learn about the kidnapping ring and murder on board. It was my job, and Ace's, to make sure those news stories read solved on the closed captioning.

"What's your suspect list at now?" Ace asked as he handed me my green tea. The deck was filled with Mai Tais and cocktails, but my frazzled nerves and healing brain required a sober selection.

I pulled up the notes on my phone—my real one the police had recovered from the beach near where we'd been taken. "I still have Lafitte and First Mate Redmont.

Heels Dug In

"We never did question Cory Redmont," Ace said.

"He's right over there." I pointed at the man in full uniform standing by the limbo contestants. I'd recognized him almost as soon as I'd stepped out on the deck for some fresh air. "He's judging the contest. I thought we could speak to him afterward."

We watched him for a minute. He was calling out names in a Southern accent: "Next up, we have Sarah from Ohio. How low can you go, Sarah?"

He looked innocent enough, and the passengers certainly enjoyed his charisma. He seemed so carefree it was hard to picture him as a murderer. Ace seemed to dismiss him entirely.

"I'd like to question Damian again."

"I don't think it's likely to be Damian."

"Why not?" he asked.

"He has an alibi. Supposedly, he gave a tour to some of the British navy officers who were working the kidnapping case. He's been cooperative with everything." This was according to second officer Wendy Rackham, who had been more forthcoming since learning that we were investigators. She had personally greeted us on our return to the ship, and she had seen me to the medical ward to make sure I was all right for traveling.

"Let's not forget Damian harbored a stowaway."

I shook my head, then stopped and waited for the woozy feeling to dissipate. I put a hand to my forehead and said, "Do you want it to be him?"

"What? No, of course not."

"You're quick to make suggestions that point to him, like mentioning the fish and the navy background."

"He knew Jamison Oliver."

"But he wasn't the only one who knew Oliver was on board. We haven't even questioned his first mate, Redmont."

"I know." Ace paused. Even he heard the defensiveness in his voice.

Putting my hand on top of his, I said gently, "You told me to never let emotions cloud my judgment."

He turned his palm up so that we were holding hands. Turning toward the railing but still grasping my fingers, he glanced at me. He smiled and shook his head. Then, he stared out at the ocean.

"Things were a lot simpler before you came into my life."

"Me?" I defended.

"Yes, you. Quoting back what I say and talking reason. It's simpler when yours is the only voice in your head."

"You mean I'm in there somewhere?"

He squeezed my hand. "You're always in there."

We stood in silence for a minute. Since Ace was opening up, I had to ask him, "What was your argument with your brother about?"

Not looking at me, he said, "There was a cabin on the Jersey shore that used to belong to my grandfather. My father used to take me up there to go fishing until my mom found out about Damian's family. Damian inherited it in my father's will. He put it up for sale, but he'd rather sell it to a complete stranger than to me."

"It sounds like he was just as hurt as you by what your father did," I said.

Ace let out a short grunt. "He's the one who spent the last few years of my father's life with him."

"You had a close relationship with your father when you had him in your life, but you don't know that it was the same for Damian. You can be close to a person and not really be emotionally attached. He might have been angry to learn that he had an older son he loved somewhere else. He might have felt like he was second in his eyes."

Ace's chest relaxed as he exhaled. "You know, you're amazing, helping me sort out my family drama and keeping Ella calm yesterday. You—

"Ella," I interrupted and pulled away.

"What's wrong?"

"Where's Ella? She said she would meet us on board by 5:00 p.m. It's half-past now."

"That's not that late. It's okay. Lizzy was going to drop her off personally."

"No, you don't know Ella," I said, now walking at a fast pace toward the upper level where Lafitte's office was located. If she was missing, he was either behind it or could help find her. I was determined to find out which. "She's never been late for anything a day in her life. I don't care if we're on vacation—she's so punctual I'd set my watch to her."

"All right. You're sure Ella said 5:00 p.m.?"

"Yes."

"Then she might've gotten distracted. Maybe she ran into someone—"

"That's exactly what I'm afraid of," I said as I walked with Ace toward Lafitte's cabin office.

"Do you think Lafitte still—"

Ace's sentence fell as we neared the bow. A scream erupted. Both our heads snapped in the direction of the sound. A bright light reflected off of something on the upper deck and I had to shield my eyes. Soon enough, whatever had glinted overhead darted out of the way, and I could see movement ahead of us in the hall on our level. The woman screamed again. It was not just any woman—I recognized the banshee-like call of my old friend and rival.

No one in the world could scream bloody murder and still retain the ladylike harmonic resonance of a Southern Ella Belle. Her distress cry was intermingled with, "Get your hands off of me." When we reached her, we found her struggling against the grasp of her assailant: Pierre Lafitte.

Chapter 15

Smoking Gun

Ace tackled Lafitte, whose arm had captured a damsel acting very much in distress at the moment. Ella pulled her arm away and looked at Ace with such gratitude. I expected the words "my hero" to escape her lips. What he needed was help, not accolades. Lafitte's revolver flew across the ground in the shuffle and landed near Ella.

"Grab it!" I said.

Ella looked between the gun and me as Lafitte's eyes widened. He dealt a blow to Ace's chin and lunged for the weapon. Ella beat him to it. Grabbing at Lafitte's chest, Ace managed to pull him back.

"Wait," Lafitte cried, "this is a misunderstanding."

Heels Dug In

Damian appeared in the hallway, putting both hands up when he saw the gun. Ella swiveled around and pointed it in his direction.

"What's going on?" Damian asked.

Ace gave Lafitte one last push, then moved toward Ella, taking the weapon out of her hands.

Damian and Lafitte moved closer, but Ace aimed the gun from one to the other. The two men moved closer together.

"Ace, don't!" I said.

"I'm not going to shoot anyone, Kait," he assured me. "Just keep your hands up, both of you, and we'll keep you in custody until we reach the dock."

"Why me?" Damian asked. He stepped forward, only for Ace to swing the revolver in his direction. Falling back, Damian held his arms up high. He said in a slower, more deliberate tone, "I don't have anything to do with whatever is going on here."

"It's not Damian," I said, putting a hand on Ace's raised shoulder.

Ella clung to the wall, her dress disheveled and her mascara running. "That's right! It's Lafitte. He grabbed my wrist and dragged me here. I trusted you, you snake!"

"No! I pulled you away from danger. You must believe me! You were being targeted."

Ace aimed at Lafitte again. "By who?"

"A revolver on the upper deck. I saw the glare of a gun and pulled her away. I did not see who aimed at her."

Ace aimed the gun toward Damien.

"It couldn't have been me," he said.

He was right. He couldn't have been on the upper deck and down here this fast. Plus, I'd seen the flash of light Lafitte was talking about.

"I think they're both telling the truth," I said.

Ace lowered the gun. "Don't you think it's time you told me everything?"

Damian dropped his hands and sighed. "Lafitte, we'll use your office."

Lafitte led us a few rooms down, excused the on-duty officers, and pulled up chairs for us all. Ace preferred to stand, leaning in the doorway. Damian stood in a similar stance.

He said, "I was aware of the very first disappearance that we'd experienced, but at first we thought the issue was on the island. When the second passenger disappeared, I started speaking with island officials and my superiors at Mondragon International about increasing island and ship security. Still, I thought it was the island that wasn't safe. There was a report of a woman kidnapped near the Surfing Dragon construction sight. Then, shortly after, Emily Roberts came to me with suspicions that a couple officers on board were involved. She apparently heard them talking. Emily told my first mate, who didn't report it to me, because he wanted to substantiate the claim first. When she told me, I didn't wait. I reported my suspicions to head office when the third girl disappeared.

"But when Emily went missing, that's when I started to think that you, Lafitte, or maybe other people on board might be involved. I didn't know who to trust. So, before we set sail again, I hired my friend, Jamison Oliver, to investigate in stealth. He wasn't a stowaway—he had a ticket purchased under a different name. Once he was dead, I didn't know what to do, so I didn't say anything."

"Did anyone else know he was on board?"

"Redmont was the only other person aware of Oliver, and he knew of Emily's and my suspicions from the start. He was helping us investigate."

I looked at Ace. "You heard Redmont on the microphone, didn't you?"

Ace nodded, understanding my meaning. He said, "Emily had a boyfriend on the crew. Do you know who it was?"

Damian looked genuinely surprised. "No. This is the first I'm hearing it. Of course, if I knew I'd be dutybound to issue a reprimand. Fraternization is—"

"Not allowed. We know." I was tired of hearing about the taboo of workplace romances.

"I'm lost," Ella said. "Are you trying to say Redmont knew who Emily's boyfriend was? Was he involved in the murder onboard? Or the kidnappings?"

"Both," I said. "Redmont has a Southern accent. Emily's boyfriend had an accent. Redmont knew Oliver was on board and his real purpose in coming. Oliver was killed, and it was made to look like the captain was the target. Lafitte had a motive to target the captain if he was involved in the kidnappings, which is what we started to think when Ella became the target."

"So, Redmont planned everything?" Ella asked.

"Except killing Oliver," Lafitte said. "He was on navigation duty at the time."

"He could have poisoned the fish anytime from preparation to delivery. He had a motive if Oliver was on to him," Ace said.

"There's a simple way to prove he's guilty of both the kidnapping and the murder," I said.

"What's that?" Damian asked.

"Even a shark can be reeled in with the right bait."

Chapter 16

Bait and Catch

Ella didn't prefer to be bait for a killer and kidnapper, but I convinced her she would be all right. With the captain and the second mate, Wendy, in on it—and Lafitte ready to protect her at the first sign of trouble—she agreed to play the part.

Wendy set up the video camera and audio relay in Redmont's room. Then she bound Ella's hands and tied her to a chair. We waited. His shift over, Redmont arrived within fifteen minutes. Clicking on the light, his eyes widened.

"Hello, sir."

"Wendy? What is this?" he feigned innocence.

"This is me wanting in on the action. I know you've been kidnapping those girls, and I know you're after this one." She pushed Ella's shoulder, and Ella gave a terrified squeal—as much as she could through the duct tape over her mouth.

"You're insane, I'm calling for help." Cory reached for the wall phone.

"You already have a fall guy. I've drugged Lafitte. He won't wake till morning—he'll have no alibi," Wendy pressed.

Cory kept the receiver in his hands. He put his finger on the hook switch, seemingly considering what to do. He set down the phone.

"I don't know what made you think I want in on this, but I don't. I'll tell that police that it was you unless you let the girl go."

In Lafitte's office, I asked, "Were we wrong?"

"He's not taking the bait," Ace said.

"He is too smart. He will not fall for this," Lafitte said.

"Wendy is smart, too," Damian said.

We focused our attention back on the video.

"It's too late for that," Wendy said. "This woman overheard your man, Bowen, calling you by name, 'Cory.' She put it together after you shot at her. Her friend, Kait, mentioned your name. Suddenly, she's coming to me, as a fellow woman, with 'I don't know who to trust' and 'I think it's Cory Redmont behind all this.' We may have to take her friend out, too."

"And then what? Take out her friend's husband and the captain and Lafitte?"

"You had no problem with Oliver. They have no way to prove that was you."

He was silent a minute, unsure whether to trust her. She took a switchblade from her belt, the metal dug into Ella's neck. The fear on her face was palpable when Wendy drew blood.

I looked at Ace. He put a hand on my arm, reassuringly. She had me convinced she was ready to kill Ella. Damian notice my expression.

"Don't worry. I know. Wendy is a better actress than I thought, but she is acting."

She acted well enough that Redmont said, "Not like that. Wait."

He went to the television set on a small entertainment cabinet. Sliding the cabinet over, he held his hand out for Wendy's blade. She handed it to him.

He felt the wall and made a small cut. The camera Wendy had set up was placed inside a vent over the bed. From its position, we couldn't see what he was doing.

Wendy described it. "A secret compartment? You re-plastered the wall?"

He reappeared in the camera's line of sight. "I like to have a spare bit of poison on hand."

"What is it?"

"Tetrodotoxin."

"Pufferfish poison?"

"It's less messy than other forms of poison."

"We could say she broke in. Like you did with Oliver."

"And what happened with that? Think, Rackham. They suspected the captain. No, she has to be far away from my cabin."

He walked closer to Ella.

"We have to stop it," I said.

"No," Damian said. "He hasn't confessed to anything yet."

"He's as much as said that—"

"'As much as said' is not the same as saying it," Damian insisted.

"He's going to kill her. I can't let this go on." Lafitte lifted the walkie-talkie.

"Wait," Ace said. "Look."

Redmont had taken the covering from Ella's mouth to administer the poison, she screamed, and Wendy covered her mouth.

"Don't scream or we'll have to do this the hard way," Wendy said, then she released her.

Heels Dug In

"You won't get away with this. I'm not like Oliver, people know I'm on board," Ella insisted.

"Oliver said the same thing. He said Damian knows I'm on board, he'll investigate and find me out. But I disposed of every trace of my involvement with Emily— even the letter Oliver found. She just had to put that in the ship's mail for her parents. And I told her not to write about me."

"So you killed her like you're going to kill me?" Ella said with a mix of fear and disgust.

Redmont pointed the blade at Ella. "No, girl, you're different. She never actually knew it was me with the kidnappings. She may have suspected, but she didn't know. So, I got rid of her, I didn't kill her."

"What does that mean?" Ella asked.

"She's on another island, isn't she?" Wendy asked.

"Yes, and that's all you need to know." It was clear Redmont still wasn't sure he could trust Wendy. But he was ready to use her help to get rid of Ella.

"Hold her head back," he said to Wendy.

"We have enough," Lafitte said. He lifted the walkie-talkie. "Move now." And he ran out the door.

Wendy hadn't held Ella down, so Redmont stood, advancing on her. Lafitte's men surrounded him. He swung for Wendy, but she deflected. Lafitte barged in, pushed Redmont against the door, and cuffed him.

Wendy untied Ella.

"Sorry about your neck," she said, handing her a wad of tissues from the nearby nightstand.

Ella pressed them against her neck. "At least I'm alive."

Over the walkie-talkie, Lafitte said, "We got them."

Damian pressed the button back. "We're on our way."

Ace and I didn't follow him, however. We contacted Lizzy, who informed us of the good news: Bowen had struck a deal under questioning. He'd given away the location of the girls. They were alive. And they were going home.

***

Our call to room 2201 the night before meant the Roberts wanted to have breakfast with us the next morning. There was no reason for delaying departure in the morning, as Redmont was taken off and the evidence was handed over to the officials on the island before the night was out. Mr. and Mrs. Roberts did not want to continue the journey by boat once they discovered their daughter was alive. But they insisted on seeing us before we departed.

Heels Dug In

Mr. Roberts shook Ace's hand, and Mrs. Roberts hugged me.

"How can we ever thank you?" Mrs. Roberts said.

"It wasn't us," I said.

Ace added, "The navy and the police found her."

"But they wouldn't have done it without your help," Mr. Roberts pointed out.

Mrs. Roberts agreed. "We looked you up. You have quite a reputation. We knew when we met you that you would find her."

"You know," Mr. Roberts said, "these are just the kind of stories we publish: crime novels." He reached around his pockets and handed Ace his card. "If you ever want to make your story into a book, call us."

The Fire on the Sea blared its horn, announcing departure. The Roberts hurried off to reunite with their daughter, and Ace and I began our journey home.

Chapter 17

Home Sweet Home

It was sweet to be on home soil again. Ace dropped me off at home and walked me to my door, holding his jacket over his head to shield me from the New York rain. Of course, it was raining—nothing like gray skies to greet us after the perfect weather of paradise. My heels sank into the wet ground until we hit the stone walkway that led to my house.

I could see a light flick off inside. Once we were huddled together under the arch covering the doorway, I could hear voices, too. They quieted after a minute.

I turned to Ace, holding onto him as I scraped the mud off my heels. I said, "We're not alone. Looks like they've got a welcome home party waiting inside."

Heels Dug In

As I let go of Ace and put a hand on the doorknob, he pulled me back.

"Kait, I have something to say."

"Can't it wait? I want to find out my exam scores."

I was cold, exhausted, and soaking wet. Plus, he'd had the whole car ride to tell me what was on his mind and hadn't said two words. All he'd done was stare out the window.

I'd given up on conversation halfway in, calling Scarlett instead. She'd listened to the details of our travel, which had been all over the news. In the excitement of our catching an international kidnapping ring, I had forgotten to ask about my exam scores.

Ace said, "I already know what they say."

"You do?"

"Perfect score—or close, knowing you."

I laughed. "Let's hope so." I turned, but his arm didn't leave my waist. I felt a shiver rush through me. This time it wasn't the cold.

Turning to look at him, I saw the warmth in his eyes and relaxed into his grip. He glanced at my lips, leaned in, and stopped as if struggling. My hands found their way to his shoulders and I pulled closer.

"You had something to say?" I asked.

He searched my eyes until he found the courage to speak. "Yes. Something I wanted to say this whole time, but I didn't know how."

"Go on," I said.

He brushed my hair away from my face. "I wanted to be sure. I didn't want to hurt you or get hurt myself. I didn't want our relationship to be a fling or something we regretted later."

"That's why you said we were on hold until I got my PI license? I thought that was you worrying about our boss/employee relationship."

He smiled. "Let's be honest, we've been equal partners in all but name since you started."

I looked away, exaggerating a shrug with my shoulders. "There is the question of salary."

He chuckled. "Then let's split this last one equally. Sound fair?"

"I did put my life in danger—how about sixty-forty?"

He laughed and put out a hand. "All right. Deal."

I shook on it. "Good, because I already spent it."

He titled his head, but he didn't ask. Instead, he looked at the ring on my finger and raised my hand to his lips. I felt my heart stop, resuming only when his eyes staring into mine brought it back to life.

Heels Dug In

"Kait, I want us to be partners, not just in work, in—" he paused.

"In love?" I asked.

He smiled. "In everything."

I smiled slyly. "Are you proposing that I keep this ring?"

"No."

My jaw dropped. "No?"

He pulled a jewelry box out of his pocket. "I was hoping you'd accept this one."

He opened it to reveal a double row of diamonds on a silver band.

"The ring from Zazbry's," I said, marveling at the fact that he must have purchased it before the trip.

He bent down on one knee.

"So?" he asked.

"So? Ask me the whole question."

He chuckled. "Kaitlynn Amelia Sasse, will you marry me?"

I took out a key from my pocket. "If you accept this. I was going to wait until the right time to tell you, but I think this works as an engagement present." Ace looked confused, glancing at the key. I smiled. "I convinced Damian to sell the cabin to the right person."

"You bought it?"

"No. Actually, I used some of the money Lizzy paid us as a down payment and had him write up a draft with your name on it. If you still want it, he's willing to sign. The keys are an extra set. He lent them to me so we could take a look at it."

He took them into his hand and glanced down. I couldn't see his face, but I hoped he was smiling. I said, "There is one stipulation. Damian would like you to invite him to go fishing at least once. He'd like to get to know his brother."

He beamed. His eyes were shining when he looked up at me. I was touched to see him so close to tears. He joked to cover the emotion. "I accept. Now, will you give me your answer so I can get off my knee?"

I laughed, but it came out as a half-choked "yes," as I realized that I was on the verge of tears. Ace stood up and drew me in for a kiss: deeply, passionately, perfectly.

Though we didn't want to pull away, we had a house full of friends with whom we should share the news. We went inside. I flicked the light on. The sight of all my friends, my godmother, Scarlett, and Ace's friends, his mother, and his sister and her family greeted us. A huge banner read: *Congratulations*. All of our friends shouted the same.

Heels Dug In

Before I could show off my new ring, I realized this wasn't an engagement party.

Scarlett stepped forward. "Congratulations to the two PI's in the room, or the 'High Seas Heroes,' as they've been calling you on the news."

She handed me the envelope with my exam scores. It hadn't been opened. She just had enough confidence in me to have me find out my scores in front of everyone. If I hadn't passed, this would become less of a party and more like a therapy session.

"Open it," Ella insisted. She already had a glass of champagne to celebrate.

Taking a deep breath, I ripped open the envelope and looked at the numbers. Ace was right. It wasn't perfect, but it was close.

"Oh, I knew it." Scarlett gave me a hug.

Ella gave me a smirk. "Congratulations. I knew it would happen eventually."

I smiled. "Thanks."

"By this time next year, you'll be a full-fledged PI," Ace added.

"I was referring to the ring on her finger," Ella said, taking a sip of her drink. "I knew you two would get there."

"Thanks," Ace and I both said.

Congratulations came from around the room, and Ace and I exchanged hugs and handshakes with everyone until I circled back to Ella. I found her over by the cake. She hadn't yet taken a piece, so I cut one and handed it to her.

"It's going to happen for you one day soon, Ella. I'm sure of it," I said as she accepted the slice.

"So am I," she said. "For once in my life, I'm digging my heels in and standing up to my father. Diamond Springs is not a money mill; it's a community. I'd like to be friends again, Kait." She offered a hand.

I pulled her into a hug. "Friends."

She tried to pull away, then she thought better of it and returned the gesture. I had no more "frenemies" in Diamond Springs, only friends. It was a good feeling.

I'd felt lost traveling the world as a model. I missed the feeling of family I'd felt here more than anywhere else. I came to Diamond Springs to live in a place where I could feel like I belonged. And with good friends like Ella, Ava, and Victoria, a godmother like Scarlett, and a fiancé like Ace, I was glad to be home.

Want more great content?

Hi, I'm Astoria Wright, the author of A Sassy Sleuth's Mystery series. I hope you've enjoyed Book 3: Heels Dug In.

Check out the rest of
A Sassy Sleuth's Mystery series:
Hot on the Heels
Head Over Heels
Heels Dug In

Check out Astoria Wright's other series,
The Faerie Apothecary Mysteries:
Chaos in the Countryside
Herbs and Homicide
Remedy and Ruins
Elixirs and Elves
Charms and Changelings
Potions and Panic
Talismans and Turmoil
Tonics and Turning Points

To keep up-to-date about this series and others by the author, check out the website:

www.astoriawright.com

Sign up for the mailing list for updates and freebies available only to members!

Thanks for reading!

THE KILLING OF PERRY SANTOS

It was nine thirty in the morning when Perry Santos came outside to pick up the mail. The phone books had been delivered the day before and were in a yellow plastic bag at the foot of the mailbox. There was a bag for each house on the square, five of them, and they were all prepared for infiltration. The agents sent to monitor Santos and his movements noticed that he chose bag #2, a message was sent to the Cog in order to switch on the data conduit in bag #2.

Another message was sent to 'deflate' the magnetic signal in the other four bags. Now that Perry had taken the magnetic capture into his living space, his emails and phone chatter and almost every move made in the building could be monitored thoroughly. In each plastic bag a tiny smear of silicon dust held a magnetic signal; the agents at the Cog could use this to expand upon the carbon displacement signature. The signature could be untwined to reveal even the emotions of each word he spoke. In a manner of speaking, his metaphysical incarceration had just begun. When the Cog decides to put the hood on you, it is only a matter of time before it drives you to insanity or you are killed.

Santos drew the attention of his neighbors some time ago, his scheduled arriving and leavings became erratic in regards to his work schedule. The neighbors grew in their suspicion; there were other small incidents that caused him to be alerted for surveillance. The magnetic signatures could be applied to an individual but there has not been a discovery of how to remove that signature. Once this yoke was laid upon one's shoulders, it could not be removed.

Mindy Boyle was assigned to oversee the application process. Her team was assembled from a retinue of the most solid Carbon Signature Technologists available. They even gave her Lance Harnish, the professional impostor, to help infiltrate Perry Santos and his life.

Within a few hours, the Santos household was under complete capture. Perry and Vanessa went out for coffee in the morning. Boyle nodded at Captain Orton. Team 9 from the Cog moved in quietly and set enough hooks to catch the specific fish they were hungry for.

Perry's children were away at boarding school in New Haven. the 3 of them were being tracked and recorded in a similar manner. This was a secondary measure that was in place to detect any 'overspill' of the transfer of sensitive data. It was the hope of the directors at the Cog to gain the information Mr. Santos might let slip, either consciously or subconsciously.

Perry had been a part of a languages team for the State Department. The group he was in was used to discover a message in a Greek embassy communiqué that revealed ominous details regarding an assassination plan. The sensitive nature of the plan caused a great deal of strain in the intelligence community; several "groups" were formed to work the investigation without oversight.

There was one official group whose activities were reported in full and documented for release to the press and to the public at large. Opposed to that, there were a number of other teams whose findings were not reported, they were kept under wraps completely. The secrecy required in this situation grew from the crossing of alliances in the intelligence community. To be found out would jeopardize many gains in the diplomacy game.

Perry was the archivist and interpreter for one of the covert groups. Santos and his entire group was out on loan to one of the private intelligence corporations across the pond. Lerner Tri-Corp paid much better than the government, in the orientation it was explained like this;

"Should a member of the group be contacted by an outside party in order to be co-opted for useful information, Lerner Tri-Corp will triple the amount of that offer to keep the information in house. Alert your Case Director to any offers or discussions that come about on this subject. Refusal to agree to this principle is grounds for immediate disposal."

The team was solid and reliable but LTC understood the limits of human integrity. It was safer to acknowledge these faults and provide protection against betrayal in the knowledge of these limits. In a few months, the work was complete. Assassins in seven countries were detected and removed, the message was destroyed and Perry's group was dissolved. The project ended and now the cleaning up could begin.

Members of the team had to follow a protocol to ensure secrecy; one member per day could be driven to an airstrip outside of Helsinki. The member was packed into a cargo box outfitted for safe human travel. The box contained a cot and a sitting area where a trunk of refrigerated drinks and food could be accessed. Once secure inside the cargo box, it was loaded into the hold of a C-130 and flown over Greenland and the Hudson Bay to a remote base in rural Manitoba. The C-130 would touch down in the dark of night, on a slice of land in the middle of Lake Winnipeg. Rowing ashore, they were given travel documents and their final payments. The member would then be taken to Toronto by car and given their release from the company. In most cases the member would arrange their own travel back home from Toronto. After these precautions, the members were on their own, all records of their work or participation were erased.

Perry was the last to leave; his wife was relieved when he finally made it home to Bridgeport. She anguished alone as he had left in mysterious circumstances in the middle of the night. He asked her for complete trust and was vague about when or if he would return. Having been home for a week and a half now, they resumed a normalcy in their dialogue. She couldn't be told anything about his work, Perry was a bad liar. It was best to never bring it up, even though she was dying to know. Perry understood the possibility of people listening in, he would not talk about his work out loud anywhere.

There was little activity in the Santos home that morning. The agents in a truck nearby began to detect that there were two individuals in the house, both were laying in a supine position, perhaps sleeping in a little longer. The data capture was in full progress.

In the quiet Connecticut countryside, a black Jaguar XJ-12 blurred past the groves and green shrubs, past a flat-bed truck, then descending into a valley with no resistance. Thirty miles from Bridgeport, Ellen Albright checked her GPS again before pulling over to confirm her appointment with Perry.

"You've reached the Santos family; we are out at the moment and will return your call as soon as we- BEEP"

Ellen made sure the beep stopped before talking, "Mr. Santos, this is Ellen Albright with Archer-Green Realty and I was hoping we still had an appointment at noon today" She ended the call, turned the radio back up and continued through the overgrown valley. Fifteen miles out, Perry called back.

"Hi Ellen, I am here so you can come earlier if you'd like to"

Ellen was not in a hurry but she had motivation to free up time for her own purposes later on. "I can be there in about thirty minutes, Mr. Santos?"

"That would be great; we'll put on some coffee"

The tone was perfectly transmitted through Agent Danny Weaver's headset. The whole team caught the conversation completely. The digital signal of every electronic device in the house was now on the transom of at least three dozen agents working for The Cog.

A calculation of email contacts to messages sent provided the algorithm to snare two possible co-conspirators.

Inspector Daniels gave a note to Boyle, "Mindy, take a look at this"

"A junior high school yearbook photo? Who is this?" Mindy asked.

"It's Miss Albright, from a different time, her name back then was Rothstein.......and look across the page here..." Daniels was meticulous to point Boyle to the clincher.

"Perry M. Santos, that's the connection?" Boyle was livid that this bit of information had been overlooked. "They were childhood friends? This makes no sense, why would she be involved in the delivery of materials?"

Inspector Daniels asserted his knowledge from here; "She was co-opted four years ago when the CIA found she was on hard times. They used her for a decoy to draw out double-dealers." Daniels continued, "When they found out she knew Santos the decision was made to bring her in."

"Does she know of our presence here?" Boyle didn't miss a detail.

"No, she has no clue that we are watching, her obligations ended when the Project was dissolved."

"Let me get this straight, my team is going to take out a neutral target, a civilian?" Boyle was repugnant to the idea.

"Director Boyle, you don't have to take anybody out unless materials are transferred, I think Miss Albright sort of leaves the 'civilian' realm right about that time" Inspector Daniels had a point.

"Call the interpreter in, in case he goes into Portuguese with Albright." There would be no cracks for information to slip through.

The Cog was protecting an inner agent, a double-agent really. The names that Santos and his team were working in their investigation were mostly benign nomenclatures that bore no reality. Unfortunately, one name- the most sensitive name that could be revealed was found in a batch of their lead suspects. The Cog works in between all the international agencies, they work in a hidden capacity. The CIA, Interpol, and the New KGB have no idea that The Cog even exists. In fact, without the help of The Cog, none of those agencies could exist for very long.

"Get Keegan on the line for me, now. I actually meant yesterday…" Boyle was on the hunt now, a raised head would be summarily chopped off without even a blink in the eyes.

"Professor Keegan, this is Ann Ryan from

Fulton Industries, I was wanting to know if you could open your email and take a look at some writings for us…" Mindy gave her eyes a rub behind the dark frame glasses.

After a brief discussion, she had whatever data was required to pull the trigger on Ellen and her contact.

"Red Dog Blitz on One." She announced the decision.

With that salutation, Mindy walked out of the rear of the paneled truck and got into a long black Cadillac, she was whisked away before the buttons were pressed on a pack of C-4 under the floors the Santos home. The road team got behind Ellen's car a few miles outside of town. She heard the explosion coming from the Santos house several miles out. Soon the smoke was rising; fire trucks were called ahead of time to reduce further civilian casualties. Only Perry was killed, his wife was lucky to have been walking up the stairs at the time, she was injured quite seriously. Agents from the Cog would enter the house and finish 'exploding' her.

On the highway near Bridgeport Connecticut, agents pursued Ellen's car immediately. In moments there were three cars beside hers, she had to pull over.

As Ellen looked into the rear-view mirror, she was overcome by goose-bumps of the very worst variety. She rolled down the window knowing that there was no use in running from the Cog, she never thought they would kill her right there on the road in front of everybody in broad daylight. A shadow-gray figured approached, it was faceless behind a wool mask. The gun was raised to her ear and she smelled the still burning gunpowder, it was clear to her that this weapon had just been used. The heat of the barrel was scorching against her skin, she jumped at the pain. The figure stood quietly, like a statuesque representative of impending death. The orders were to not shoot until the target spoke.

"Am I in-

Her head flew back and her neck was bleeding, all human sense left her countenance. As blood was running down the door, her head was resting now against the opened window.

Mindy Boyle was off to catch another plane to finish the European leg of the cleanup job. She stood with two agents inside the ticket office of the private hangar.

"Get me Daniels, YESTERDAY!!"

In a few moments, a suited male secretary handed her a phone and an earpiece.

"Daniels, nice work. Can you meet me in Helsinki tomorrow? I have more work for you."

It wasn't clear whether he answered in the affirmative or not, she set the earpiece down and started to undress while she changed her clothes. Mindy wasn't bashful as she stood, boobs out for all to see, demanding the rest of the Helsinki files. Once she had been appropriately costumed, she walked out onto the tarmac towards the charter for Finland.

"Agent Carroll, do you think I have nice tits?"

"Yes Ma'am, perky too for a woman of your age."

"I knew I could count on you Carroll."
"Yes Ma'am, have fun in Disneyland"

IRON SPRINGS ROAD

The four streetlights down the dead end of Iron Springs Road clicked on as the grips of a long dusk advanced into evening. Several children played in the common area between the corner houses. They were becoming silhouettes, animated in less and less detail as the darkness ebbed closer. Out of this serene and complacent scene, the voice of Mrs. Quiroz called out for the two boys she resentfully fed around this time every night. As the boys turned and ran towards home, I decided that I would head home and wash up for dinner too.

My mother was still asleep in her chair, where I'd left her around 3 O'clock.

"Mom, hey, wake up!" With the slightest of shakes she came to and realized there was little time left to make dinner. The phone rang.

Without leaving her chair, she was able to reach behind her and grab the receiver from the cradle.

"Yeah, hon… I haven't started dinner yet… just getting ready to." she was obviously interrupted. "You want to do that tonight?" She announced dismay with whatever scheme my father was cooking up. This political play gave her the onus to order pizza and blame it on unexpected company.

I was too curious; knowing the crazy assortment of salesmen my father had invited to our house over the years, something interesting would happen in our house tonight, I just *had* to know what it was.

"Is dad on his way home?" I asked in a knowing tone.

"Yes, he will be here shortly, he is having the floor people to the house later. Would you like to go to Kimmy's for the night?" she often tried to pawn me off on Aunt Kimmy, especially on these evenings where company was expected.

"Nah, I'd rather stay here and help pick out the tiles for the floor." My request was made to sound earnest because the prospect of going to Aunt Kimmy's held little appeal. I honestly did not care one tick as to which coverings they decided upon.

After their customary kiss, dad swept past me on the way up to his room to change. He gave an impression that he'd barely made it home in time to meet the visitors. The three of us sat down and ate. I nibbled cautiously at my first slice while my father kept all alertness towards the front room window. The curtains had been tied back in a crude fashion. Somewhere into my second slice, as I picked a flake of anchovy off the top of a pepperoni, a van pulled up outside.

It was non-descript with no logo on the side, when the driver got out and opened the back panel to retrieve a briefcase, 'Ransom's Flooring' read plainly in calligraphic font across the shiny opened door. As the two men approached the front door, my mother rolled into the foyer to greet them letting them in through the screen door. The second man stopped in the doorway, preventing the tell-tale squeak that sings out the finality of the front screen-door returning home. I could hear the door ease to its stop even though I could not see the entry way from the dining room.

Laughing gregariously as most of these salesmen do, my father took them into the den and showed them the blueprints for our house. An unnecessary charade, he did this to clarify what work to do, and where it needed doing. By showing them the prints, he asserted a role of 'Creator', not easily persuaded to pay for unsolicited work. As per custom, they were warned to stay away from the "Sitting Room" at the end of the long hallway. No reason given, just the injunction to avoid entering. I sat outside the archway to my father's den and listened.

He says, "We can go measure these rooms, I already measured them but I would like you to verify them."

The shorter of the two men went off to do just that, while the taller, extra-tanned fellow stayed with dad. When the guy came back from measuring the rooms, he said that there was only one discrepancy. Shaking his head, he asked us all to come look at it. Dad liked to double check the work, so eagerly he went with tape in hand.

"One of the rooms is four feet longer than you have it reported, probably my mistake." As we all walked into the sunken living room area, Dad took out the tape.

"You have 22 feet along the sides of the room; you had it down as 18."

Dad looked at the squat fellow with confusion. Ten years prior, my parents had this house built from blueprints that they had toiled over for years. I was just a baby then; don't remember much more than the smell of fresh paint and sawdust from that time.

Without even walking over to measure my father could, and did insist that the floor could only be 18 feet, based on the exterior dimensions of the room. Taking a tape to the corner and measuring along the back of the kitchen wall, his tape read 22 feet.

"This can't be...I know this room is 18 feet long, I designed it myself!"

Frustrated, he went to the other side of the room, 22 again.

"Darrr-Laaaa!" he sang out for my mom to come in.

"Do you remember the length of this room as we drew it up?" he asked her knowingly.

"18 feet, because of the size of the tiles from what I recall..." She was not yet privy to the weirdness we were watching unfold.

"Okay, go outside and measure the wall outside this same room." Dutifully, they all went out and set the tape down by the corner, and the taller salesman announced, "19 feet 6 inches" Dad was right. This could not be. They looked at everything. They measured for a rise in the foundation, even a sighting stick was used to determine the calibration for surveying. These numbers were holding up, Dad was now horribly out of his element.

"How can a room grow four feet on the inside?" and then I heard the short guy stop thinking about it. I felt it was because he was entering an area of supposition that proved too daunting. A solution well beyond the scope of his reasoning. My young mind felt a wave of awareness to something odd that was happening in regards to the space of this room. Suddenly, Dad could worry no longer over floor coverings.

The four adults sat around the kitchen table and drank coffee while debating the next move.

"I am calling an engineer tomorrow, when we find out what's going on, we'll have you guys back out for a re-measuring". After a comical discussion of the strange sights they'd witnessed. Mom suggested that there could be an angular explanation which was not seriously acknowledged. Dad thanked them for their time, apologized for not having time left to discuss the flooring transaction. The bewildered men walked out the front door, stymied at the occurrence they had just been a part of.

When I woke the next morning, there was a flurry of voices and footsteps coming from downstairs. I had dreamed vividly for a second or two before my eyes opened. Dreaming that I woke up at school and the din below was the crowd moving through the hallway. Going downstairs I noticed that Mom had made three large pitchers of coffee, which were still smoking hot.

A bunch of men in coats were milling about, one woman in a blue lab coat was directing everyone. Dad saw me and I was scolded away to safety, as if I'd walked into a fire. I listened from the hallway;

"There are four additional feet inside this room that cannot be found outside the room, Mr. Drayton." The woman spoke in a broken accent, either Spanish or German. I think she was from the college.

"How can four feet just appear suddenly?" He stumbled, "you'll have to pardon me, this seems impossible....." Dad didn't understand quite exactly what was going on.

I guess when I had gone to bed last night, Dad stayed up working on this. There was a platoon of strange lab coats walking around. Mom was exhausted and I was too, neither one of us slept well. A surveyor crew arrived and Dad directed them to measure the outside from every point of sight. After a time, they all gathered in the den.

"Mr. and Mrs. Drayton, we are grateful that you have called us in to decipher this spatial phenomenon, there are still no clear answers to why there is more space inside the room than the outside should allow."

Suddenly from the living room there was a buzzing sound. We hurriedly moved as a group down the hallway where there was a man screaming from within the buzz. A bright flash scorched through the room and the buzz was gone. The flash had scared many of us into running out the door to the backyard.

Anxious and curious, the lady in the blue coat set her clipboard down and started walking back in.

My dad met her by the door and they looked in where smoke was now billowing out. When the smoke started to dissipate, they noticed a man's body was stuck in mid-air and protruding from the wall. It wasn't a whole man. It was just the one shoulder, the neck and the head were there, as if they'd been mounted after a successful hunt. This was not one of the lab coats, it was someone who'd just appeared from nothing. He sat motionless, lifeless. His dress was old-fashioned, like maybe even out of the early 20th Century.

A lab coat came into the room, the inside now measured 18 feet as it had on the prints. His voice trembling, devout in the truth of the 18 feet.

This is where the blue coat lady ushers everyone outside.

"Possibly, there is some kind of dimensional elasticity in that room," she abruptly changed her cadence, "Not really doing any science first, I would guess that the man inside was squeezed into a temporal displacement of some kind."

The next few hours developed into even more bizarre findings. We were now trying to arouse the consciousness of our time-traveling pilgrim. Several measurements were taken since this crazy turn of events. The size of the exterior allows for 18 feet now, and the interior falls within that. Measuring commenced every 30 minutes to make sure.

The police arrived and the paramedics came to try and release this man from the wall. Cutting into the wall they discovered that the rest of this man was tatters, chemically joined into the building materials. They were able to successfully get both shoulders and most of his torso out of the wall and they laid him down on a mat that was on the floor. He was breathing but not speaking. The paramedics continued working until eventually he opened his eyes.

While he was not sure of his surroundings, he did not seem surprised. He started blinking in a deliberate fashion.

"The blinking is in a pattern like Morse code, or some kind of cipher" said Lady Blue Coat. "Who knows Morse?"

"I have a communications degree," Mom interjected, " I can read Morse code pretty well, it's been years since I've used it, I might be a little slow."

Miss Blue Coat asks mom, "Mrs. Drayton would you see if you can pick up what he is saying, he may be lucid and aware for a very short time so we need to hurry." Blue coat lady got bossy.

"He is saying… explosion in the lab, he was hurt really bad." Mom tried harder, squinting to undo her near-sightedness.

"He is part of a Time experiment in 1937.....he says…no, he is asking for Dr. Lutz, also he is asking if it's 1937, he's asking if it worked?"

The boss lady asked; "Can he hear us?" Mom nodded yes with the wall guy.

"I'm Dr. Vivian Irios sorry you are hurting Yes,

this is 1986, are you able to breathe okay?" Dr. Irios was the Blue coat lady's title, he responded to her voice. After the buzz subsided, the man was hearing fairly well. He indicated that the rest of him was still in 1937, in a wall that the people of that time were currently poking at, he could feel his legs being poked at. Dad sat in disbelief and explained to me that somehow this guy was simultaneous living in worlds at two different times, the stuff of fiction. Hollywood stuff.

Dr. Irios spoke, "Somehow an explosion created a hole in time or in the very fabric of space, it would be reasonable to assume that this was the focus of their experiments," she paused again, "ask if him if he can wiggle his toes in the other dimension?" after a small delay, he blinked in the affirmative.

Dad, who had been quietly listening to all that had gone on, was now boisterously proclaiming that this was an opportunity, not to be missed, to give the people of 1937 information, valuable information about the coming years.

Dr. Irios considered what he was saying and conversed with her colleagues briefly.

The policeman in charge of the scene was now saying we all had to leave. The Center for Disease Control and a Hazardous Materials team would need unfettered access to the scene. Also, the city was going to cordon off and quarantine the entire 2 block area. I guess there was radiation or something.

Before leaving, Dad whispered something to Mom, an admonishment of some kind. She looked dour and confused.

"Why would I tell him that?" she asked wildly.

"Just convey that message, non-verbally, and then join us out in the yard." Dad replied.

With this instruction, Mom went over to the man from our wall, still lying on the floor. She leaned down towards him and whispered and blinked until the message was received.

I asked Dad what it was that he'd wanted the man to hear.

"Manhattan Project Dire Necessity, ensure completion at all costs"

Having accepted the message, he wiggled his toes in Morse code to the people in 1937. This went back and forth, he was being asked to confirm his identity in 1937, bureaucracy is a bitch even between dimensions of time, I guess. He was able to confirm that they'd received the message. At the time, I had no idea what that meant but I later learned that in 1937 there was a strong voice in opposition to beginning atomic studies. Had the powers at hand known of the need for it, they would have never been so hesitant in completing work on the Atomic Bombs that ended WWII. Though not known then what caused the work to move forward in secret, it was this message from 1986, from my Dad, that made the finishing of that "Manhattan" project possible.

A LONG AND LONELY LIFE

I take the first train from Waltham into Boston every morning. I get a thrill out of starting the day while it's still dark, I guess. Along the way I have met an assortment of every branded lunatic pretending to be from professional world.

The austere laborer passing as "Executive material", threw us all into conversation in the safety of his absence. It was low of us to do so but in a way, he called for it.

I will never forget the time that a local city councilman sat reading his paper quietly, the buzz of the tracks humming underneath. He cringed with every atom in his being when the king of all hoboes plunked down next to him. The smell must have been too much, the young politician stood up, never losing focus on his paper. He tried in vain to not acknowledge this intrusive act, but he was revealed as a narcissist when his stop came.

"You really need to take a bath Sir; until you do you should stay away from those of us still clinging to the concept of hygiene"

He stepped out of the doors just in time to negate any response from the peanut gallery. I for one kept silent though, I would have snickered sarcastically being from the outskirts of London, by way of Cambridge.

I also remember that morning; I was riding past the Olympic Avenue station in order to grab a lunch bag from Costa's Deli. It so happened that a very pretty girl walked off the train the same time as I did, we bumped into each other when she knelt down in front of me to tie her boots up. That was a lie, I purposely ran over her as she had somehow suddenly blurred my common sense. I didn't yet know why but I followed her almost out of instinct.

"Oh, sorry!" I exclaimed as I clumsily fell forward over her back. My coffee went everywhere, including down the back of her skin tight blouse. The stain would not be easy to get out, I was drinking Sumatra.

"Yow!" Her voice was raspier than I'd expected, she was around five feet tall; maybe five foot two. Her physical plant belied the large raspy voice coming out of her mouth. I almost looked for the ventriloquist behind her, it was that odd sounding.

"I am sorry Miss, that shirt is ruined. Can I help you at all?" I felt horrible about not watching my step, as well as the subsequent scalding of her shoulder blades.

"I hope you didn't get burned too bad, the coffee

is an hour old" I was so regretfully concerned that I hadn't seen the fact that she was also pregnant.

She wasn't very far along yet, just enough to indicate that she wasn't just putting on weight, a visible distortion of her shape was at play.

"That's okay, I was dumb to stop right there but if I took one more step I would have tripped on these laces anyway." She was very congenial to release me of my guilt. Most likely she had assessed me as 'creepy foreigner dude'.

I looked every bit of 29, and most of 30. I knew she found me to be askew from the design of her attraction. Frankly, I thought she was a lesbian by all appearances. But, the belly full of pitter-patter?

Just then my phone rang; she noticed my fumble as I retrieved it from deep within the vest-pocket of my jacket.

"Excuse me, one moment and I'm so sorry again. That shirt must be cleaned professionally, let me take care of that." I heard the words come out and regretted them quickly, before she spoke back.

"What, you want me to give it to you? I'm not taking my shirt off mister."

"No, I believe I misspoke, I meant to say that I have an account at Felman's Dry Cleaning, if you take it there they will repair and restore it to proper wearing condition. Sorry for the confusion." I was appallingly red in the face.

In the moment that I flipped the phone open, I experienced to my soul, a heavenly fragrance unknown to me by name.

The names of delicate birds must encompass the graceful image of this fragrance. It bore its message faintly, lightly reminding me of the sweeter notes of Swiss aristocracy. It had a bold edge that gave me pause. The essence achieved the freshness of a rose without floweriness. Before a second could pass, the screen of the phone still not lit up, the young romantic inside me delighted as he never imagined he could at the grassy highlands of an imaginary boyhood.

The aromatic seduction being unintentional on her part, as it entered me the scent became something else.

I dreamt of its glorious body and the cloud of air that each sensual pulse of it became. I felt every foggy tendril forming into needles of thinly assembled hands and fingers that would lovingly caress each molecule within my respiratory and olfactory universe. I was literally transformed into a hopeless romantic on that day, in that very moment. Her face was not of the most petite nature, the cheeks were full but not puffy. Her eyes told the archetype for every desire I'd ever known. Though my rapture within her was sold to me in entirety, my grief began likewise in that very second.

The distance between my eternal beloved and I, would evoke a steel resolve around my respect and honor from that day forth. I closed the unanswered phone and looked at her seriously. I apologized like an English gentleman, my Cambridge origin rising to the surface as I asked if it were possible to have a cup of coffee with me. I offered to pay for the blouse and she declined with possibility of a rain check for both.

"If you are willing to pay for my blouse then, yes,

I will call you soon and we can meet for coffee."
She was astutely guarding her boundary.

She nodded at me and handed me a flyer that was
promoting a place called Patrenos Obstetric Clinic
in Pawtucket, I didn't have time to read much of it
as I wrote my name and number. She rode the train
all night to get here from Pawtucket, this girl who
smelled like the heaven I was born in.

I thanked her while being as gracious and
harmlessly comical as I could possibly manage. I
was going to learn every street and byway in
Pawtucket on the quick.

This young lady entranced me; I watched every
square of linoleum that her feet chose to walk out of
my sight upon. I was jealous of the very surface of
the floor, to have been burdened by the pressure of
her heel. Never in my silent life had I experienced a
calm insanity such as this.

The crowd saw me laugh hysterically for three or
four minutes out loud. Then I wept for a good five
to ten minutes more, in the presence of strangers, in
a train station past Olympic. My emotions were
being let go in a succession of blubbering snot, I
was pathetic and yet, I was not ashamed.

I swore my love for that nameless girl
extravagantly to the heavens, against the might of a
maddening crowd in the hallways of Perplex
Station. I leapt forth out of the stairways and up into
the street, I marched broadly and with confidence
anew. My barriers previously yoked had all been
sent to the horizon, defiled without passion.

The woman had, with her delicious powders
defeated every resistance I could have for loving

deeply, unabashedly. I slaved in the knowledge that all my work; all my writings would reflect the courage of my love for this invisible lady.

She was but once seen and then sent into the Siberian wilderness of my heart.

The smell however, remained pure and clear in my nostrils.

Unfortunately it was a lifetime before she called. Over a year had passed, yet that fragrance kept me alive- that I may embrace this beautiful woman. Every strange number was answered; I kept a vigil at the window of my phone.

I think she tried to call once but then chickened out. The night she did decide to call, I was forty minutes into a double-date that was just reaching the unbearable limits of my cooperation.

I excused myself to go smoke a cigar outside on the balcony. The three companions of my evening giggled away their metropolitan guilt, listening loudly to what I would categorize as the latest in a long line of whispering femme male singers. The kind of music where they are almost insisting that they shall be seen as the "new machismo". This masculine vulnerability is just so odd to an Englishman. We understand the fact that almost every single human has at least one "gay" bone in their body, it is not even an embarrassing trait. It is life in the savannas; the social jungle is blazed with trails that lead to odd intimate behaviors. American avarice is blind to the helplessness we have on that score.

"Jack? Jack Simonds?" Her raspy voice had gained a silky finish; a new deeper tone was in her voice box.

"Yes? Who might I be speaking to?" The voice gave her dead away but playing coy might wash a little more of my perceived creepiness away. Over the years, I learned the art of demonstrating nonchalance in advance of trusting friendship.

Don't call me Mr. Simonds. God, please don't refer to me as Mr. Simonds. My heart's survival depended on the fact that she saw me simply as 'Jack'.

"This is Ana Caritolli, you might not remember me from a few months ago, we met in the station by Perplex. "What shall I call you? I wouldn't want to put you off calling you something odd like Mr. Simon or Simonds." She was a gift from the angels, I say.

It had been over a year, but I wouldn't split the hair that might cause suspicion of my deepest motives.

"My friends call me Jack, I do think I remember you, I ruined your blouse with my coffee."

I was entranced by her moist voluptuous tone. The thought of that blouse pressing against the soft pale skin, glimpsing perhaps the freckle of symbolic imperfection, everything about her voice brought her scent back to the front of my mind.

"As I recall, I owe you one blouse." I really hoped she could detect my invitation.

"And I owe you a cup of coffee; I just moved to Lynn, I was hoping to have you out this Sunday."

"I have a function on Saturday night; I will need to sleep in quite late. After that, I'm all yours." That last bit was exhibiting too much comfort; I hoped it would be swept under the carpet.

"I was thinking one-thirty?" Oh, that sweet voice, I was detecting the end of this conversation and it killed me.

"One-thirty will be perfect, where do I go?" I was all in.

"Come past Mercy to Post street, then walk towards Glenmont until you see a red clay planter on a balcony, I am flying a Dutch Soccer Flag out of the planter."

"Okay, I will take the 12:40 and see you there Sunday. Good to hear from you Ana!"

Gregarious was harmless, or so I'd been led to believe.

I now had to go once again into the breach, to help Ernie nail this girl from his tennis club. I thought her friend was cute, she was actually quite pretty. I had been spoiled on other women since that spilled coffee warmed the fragrant message that melted my heart.

The table was set for dinner, so I sat and ate my last reasonably sane meal. The night ended a few hours later when, Ernie over-stepped the comfort zone of his date. That didn't stop him from checking down to my 'date', who only slept with Ernie to revenge me somehow. Maybe he would be able to enlighten me with the sexy details of her prowess; I could not care a tinker's cuss. Tomorrow would be a crazy Saturday filled to the rim with errands and maintenances. Sunday was pretty much already here, no further preparations could be made. In the year that had passed, I waited for this moment. I began a nutrition and exercise regimen, ensuring that the universal desirability of my physical plant could not interfere with any of my intentions.

I had lost thirty pounds of fat and my face had become lean and gaunt. My wardrobe was likewise addressed. I eliminated any article of spurious clothing. T-shirts? Gone. Blue jeans? Gone.

I was going to fascinate if I did not impress. I had worked an abundance of extra accounts this past year, I was dedicated to nurturing a nest egg for this very occasion. She had taken so long that I'd managed to gather over $40,000. When I started the fund, I was insistent that I would spend all of it on our first date. That idea was not really reasonable here. I wasn't quite sure what I'd be walking into; there could be a boyfriend, a girlfriend, or worse. I knew she might have a kid by now, that would be no surprise.

I needed some books, immediately. I had long been a book junkie. A serious fix of non-fiction was in order. In the entry way of Dolby's Books, I ran into a friend from work. He invited me to sail with his brothers on Sunday, which would be to my liking any other time, but I had to decline for certain.

Another year passed before Sunday morning came, or so it seemed. I woke up at 5:20, the fictitious party that I did not attend will, however, be well reported and exaggerated for its elements regarding my subtle glories. I simply had to be the most interesting person she ever met.

I left for the station in Waltham at around 11am. I

was not going to be late for this cup of coffee. I figured that if I was too early, I could lounge about in the area and maybe find a book store to wander around in. My smart phone was able to find one paperbacks seller. Not usually my forte, I abhor romance novels, which comprise the ninety percentile of all paperback inventory, worldwide.

I seemed to keep a good enough pace to arrive at her door nervously around 1:26pm.

As I rang the bell, I was elated to see her open the door and greet me smiling.

I was anxiously awaiting a friendly embrace, from which I would be able to draw a lifetime's worth of motivation for fighting wars, writing words, and living strongly. As I was swept into the foyer of her nicely appointed row house. Two chairs at open from a table of simple crumpets and a brass decanter, very English if I was speaking honestly.

Soon I was discovering that she'd made great effort to achieve a very English setting to put me at ease, to make me feel at home.

There was the giveaway marmalade. Every person across the planet assumes that the British clamor for their marmalade. I'd actually been of a good fortune to escape its ubiquity. I did not protest the marmalade; rather, I smiled at its hint.

The smell of her skin was still as intoxicating to me as the first moment I learned of it. She wrapped her forearms around me snugly at the sides and set a dry tight kiss upon between my cheek and chin. A butterfly emerged from the invisible core of my heart, rising boldly into a visage that expressed my delight. Showing much care to absorb the affections easily, I had shaved with Lyon-St. Martinique's liniment that morning anticipating such a kiss. We sat in the cool breeze of her dining area, patio doors were held open.

"Jack, I am sorry to have waited so long to call, I was struggling to move into the city from Pawtucket. I knew I would find you once I made it here. "She had a new wisdom in her tone.

"I had not been able to forget your smell, Jack. I have thought about your smell this whole time, and you may think me rude, but can I come over there and just smell you?" My mind spun like a top with glee. Could this be?

"Jack, I was so enthralled with meeting you again that I didn't want to under-impress, I learned a lot about English stuff, I hope I did well here today with the food and such." She spoke the very mirror of my heart.

I relented as if I didn't think much of it and waved her in for a good sniff. Her chin and nose just grazed my earlobes. Her smell caused me a great sigh, the kind that communicates only one unmistakable desire. If I were to say how incredible the afternoon was, the sensual contact that took place, it would belittle the actual events. After the first few hours together, I finally inquired after the child she'd been carrying. A couple from Albany had enlisted her services as a surrogate mother, which explained her sudden personal economic boom. She had worried that I might judge that action, but I was no saint myself, I asked her to marry me before even four hours had passed. I smelled her up and down the entire time. Needless to say, we are married now; she has been my wife for twenty-seven years. I retired back to a small brick home in Cambridge last year, and she tends our garden to a proper English standard. I left my job in Boston for a private firm down in New York for the last few years of my career, Ana was insistent that didn't work past 55. The rest of my life, she said, belonged to her. Once in a while, just for fun, I spill a little coffee on her.

A VIEW FROM THE BATHROOM

This is that story you always say you're gonna write. Sitting there on the toilet, nothing good to read, you decide to try and entertain yourself.

You are a smart little fellow aren't you? The reason your mind has come to this is not important, we're here.

It isn't gonna be about the way those cold little tiles don't exactly line up in parallel symmetry, compelling as that would be.

Rather, these ten minutes of your life won't just be a verdict from the past, in the way your food has now caught up to you. You consume three pounds of food every day and give back half of that to the sewer. That is a 50% dedication to waste on a daily basis. Damned food, if you hadn't eaten so much of it, there would be no waste at all.

Hard to imagine cave men needing to wipe very

often. They probably digested and assimilated all nutrients they ever consumed; their fecal waste must have been at a minimum. You wonder to yourself, have they found old Caveman poop, and if they have, how big was it?

Hmmm. Can't stay on that subject too long.

It's time to read one of these magazines, this will be a growth period for you as there are none of your preferred periodicals in the sampling. "Modern Hedgehog Quarterly"?

Setting the magazine back down on the rack, you just remembered another facet of the Caveman civilization: no dentists. That must have sucked for the ancient Earth dweller. In some cases, there must have been such dire pain that one would consider jumping off a cliff to elude the intense levels only dental nerves can attain. You begin to understand why the olden folk would set an aged person to walk off into the wilderness to die; it was actually an act of mercy. They probably didn't have a lot of soap. When did they invent soap? You will have to Google that later. The invention of soap. Wondering intently, what year was it before humans came to a realization that body odor could be dealt with? What crazy stuff did they rub on themselves to be rid of the stink?

The first cases of Poison Ivy rash could not have been very much fun. Now that you brought it up, you notice you are getting a little ripe under the pits yourself, must check the medicine cabinet for some Right Guard.

When you came in here originally, it was to elude the conversation going on out in the Family

Room. American Idol, not really your show. Your friends like it; by default that means you like it too, at least for an hour or two a week. Where would you go without this crowd?

Come to think of it, how did you get wrapped up with these banal hooligans? Tracy you've known since 3rd Grade, Deirdre moved to Tuscaloosa a couple years later. Ryan and Chris just wouldn't go away starting in 7th grade.

Has it really come to this? You are in the bathroom hiding and taking refuge from the cultural suicide known as Television. Worse than that, you are exhausted from the same dumb conversation that has gone on for ten years now.

You need to find some new friends. Yes, a new scene of bright exciting persons, more intelligent discussions. Next Monday the search will begin for a new crowd. The pathetic existence we've cultivated runs tepid and stale now. Tonight, the world needs a new Sanjaya. The sad reflection of loserdom your friends are celebrating is but the latest in a line of rueful underdogs. It's sad that you are longing for the short talents of Clay Aiken now. Stop thinking about that show!

Okay, you are better than television and its meager offerings. What about books? You have read so many beginnings of books that you could almost be an expert on starting a book. The world needs not know that you never finished a book in your life, not even Catcher in the Rye.

Remember taking credit for that one?

That girl wasn't impressed and you thought she would be overwhelmed with adoration. There was that bus trip to Galveston when you did actually read 'Wiseguy' by Nick Pileggi, but what girl would be impressed by that?

A knock at the door and you respond that you are busy, "Bizzeee...please go upstairs to the other bathroom."

The toilet tissue for the upstairs is empty; you must do a quick wipe and then proceed to deliver a roll to the door for this intruder, only opening a crack. Your fumes are quite fierce today, safety measures must be taken. Air freshener?

Febreeze! Two quick sprays. Thirty seconds for the mist to fall, so as to avoid the look of having just sprayed the Febreeze.

You manage the wipe, fairly uneventful as you expected to see "results". Your disappointment on that score is a sign of good luck in some European countries. Where did you hear that one?

Okay, handing the roll through the door and closing it abruptly while Ryan was asking if you died in there. Stupid Febreeze, do your job!

Is it worth sitting down again?

Checking the bowl for what you assumed would appear as the Mountains of Burma, you are tricked again by three smallish clumps, just more than pellets.

You sit down again, this is therapeutic almost.

Where's that Hedgehog magazine?

Page 16: "The northern variety hedgehog relies on the seasons to attend its own self-grooming. The act is a scent-defense against the carnivorous forest population and it makes their coat smaller, which obscures it against the eyes of predatory fowl..."

Who writes this shit? Someone got paid to write that. Wow.

Page 37: "Karen Sullivan has made it her life's work to help the habitat of the northern Michigan's hedgehog population…"

Ahhhhh! You go to work for how many hours to make enough money to eek out a spaghettios and pop-tarts existence and this person lives with hedgehogs for a living?

What is this world coming to?

You realize that you just sounded like your dad; a sobering realization that sends you mentally running back into the Family Room to watch the dumbest show on TV. It might not be the pinnacle of culture, but it did signify your individuality and in a sad way it represents your time in the tumbler of the Universe. Grandpa had Bill Haley & the Comets. Dad has his Smooth Jazz and that damn Ace Of Base CD, and the Raiders of the Lost Ark movies. That was Dad's generation.

Why do you have to be saddled with 'Idol'? You were just lucky enough to get past the boy-band frenzy, now the music world is an awkward blend of hip-hoppy/uber-melodic punk. The music of an ADD generation.

Finally you were thinking well on a subject that mattered, music.

What will your children be listening to?

By then it will be three or four symphonies playing at once alongside a section of guitar noodlers. Maybe robots will take over? Too late, they already have. American Idol is a robot factory of sorts. You realize now that it is your generation causing the damage.

It wasn't enough to have one American Idol, now there are copycats everywhere. Isn't there even a Nigerian Idol show?

This world is going straight to hell and you know it.

There goes the voice of your dad again.

You'd better go reclaim your seat before Ryan comes back downstairs to sneak the beanbag away from you.